"Why a[re] my clothes? Where is everyone? Why are you here?"

"I'm here," Lukas said lowly, "because I'm the only one who came to find you. Because everyone else left before the storm hit. You're almost naked, Katherine, because if I hadn't removed your wet clothes, you would have developed hypothermia."

"You do nothing without an ulterior motive. How does helping me suit you?"

"It doesn't suit me," Lukas gritted out. "But I'm not an animal who would leave someone to die as you seem to be insinuating." He turned and took a step towards her, grey eyes offended. Angry. An icy fire burning in them. "It's your fault we're in this mess. I am the reason we made it out of that storm. So push me away." The air was slowly being sucked out of the room. "Slap me across the face and tell me to leave you." He crowded her against the wall. Katherine wasn't breathing. An electrical storm brewed in the space between them. "But you can't, can you? Because I'm the only one here."

Bella Mason has been a bookworm from an early age. She has been regaling people with stories from the time she discovered she could hold the dinner table hostage with her reimagined fairy tales. After earning a degree in journalism, she rekindled her love of writing and she now writes full-time. When she isn't imagining dashing heroes and strong heroines, she can be found exploring Melbourne, with her nose in a book or lusting after fast cars.

Books by Bella Mason

Harlequin Presents

Awakened by the Wild Billionaire
Secretly Pregnant by the Tycoon
Their Diamond Ring Ruse
His Chosen Queen

The De Luca Legacy

Strictly Forbidden Boss
Pregnant Before "I Do"

Visit the Author Profile page at Harlequin.com.

SNOWED-IN ENEMIES

BELLA MASON

PRESENTS

MIX
Paper | Supporting responsible forestry
FSC® C021394
www.fsc.org

Harlequin®
PRESENTS™

Recycling programs for this product may not exist in your area.

ISBN-13: 978-1-335-21347-1

Snowed-In Enemies

Harlequin Enterprises ULC
22 Adelaide St. West, 41st Floor
Toronto, Ontario M5H 4E3, Canada
www.Harlequin.com

HarperCollins Publishers
Macken House, 39/40 Mayor Street Upper,
Dublin 1, D01 C9W8, Ireland
www.HarperCollins.com

Printed in Lithuania

SNOWED-IN ENEMIES

All the women who have to work harder and longer for recognition

All the women who have had to prove their knowledge and passion

All the women burdened to bear the expectations of the world

This one's for you

PROLOGUE

Three years ago

THE SCREAMING REVS of V6 engines attached to cars that had more in common with a jet than anything Katherine Ward ever drove circulated around the Melbourne track. The noise, the vibration, was like a pulse in the ground. In the air. In her chest.

Katherine had made it.

All the years of study and single-minded determination had led her here: to the paddock of Alpha One. Single-seater racing was her greatest passion. A passion she shared with her father. One that she knew made him proud. And growing up, there was nothing she'd wanted more than to be an Alpha One journalist.

Now she would be doing just that.

Support cars were on track, which meant there were Alpha One drivers around who she would have to interview as the new pit lane correspondent for VelociTV. Drivers such as the world champion Lukas Jäger, who she was excited to talk to.

She could hardly control her elation. Her pounding heart. She was living her dream, and she would let nothing spoil this moment. Not even the burning anger and irritation that still lingered from earlier. Katherine had known being a woman in a male-dominated sport would be hard, but she'd hoped that good manners would prevail.

She was sorely mistaken.

Which was why she was currently in a secluded spot in the paddock, where she could breathe and find some much needed patience to deal with her VelociTV colleagues.

Katherine was the only female on the team, and she was certain if the others had anything to say about it, she wouldn't even be there. She had been excluded from the dinners at the hotel restaurant. The night before, the others had gotten a table with enough seating for only them and considering they had an uneven number of people, it must have been a deliberate arrangement. So she had sat by herself, quietly stewing until she was joined by two other women. Both of whom were Alpha One engineers, and now, valued contacts.

But it hadn't ended there. With the internet abuzz with the sexist comments made by back-marker driver Roman Poulet, conversation had been steering towards the topic for days.

'He's right,' her producer had said as he stood by the OB van earlier today. 'This sport is no place for women. I can bet you anything that the rest of the team are having to pull the weight of those female engineers.'

'Not just the engineers,' her cameraman had added, 'it's the wannabe drivers too. They don't have the strength or mental fortitude for racing.'

'Or understanding. I refuse to believe any woman could understand this sport like we can.'

Katherine had heard enough. She'd known they could see her examining the equipment that she would have to carry around as she did the day before. She hadn't been trying to hide her presence. She'd walked away then.

It had been clear they didn't want her around and being so new, there hadn't been much she could say to defend herself or any other woman in the sport. Which was why she was trying her very best to calm herself and thicken her skin. It didn't matter what they thought, she knew this sport inside out and she wasn't going anywhere.

She was just about to leave her place of refuge when her every cell went on high alert. She turned to find Lukas Jäger strolling through the paddock, chatting with Roman Poulet. The man who'd said women belonged in the home. That a woman could never physically compete with him. A man that raced for a back-marker team because he was too slow to earn a seat higher up on the grid.

All the Zen she'd attempted to achieve melted into disappointment as she watched Lukas smiling at whatever Roman was saying to him. Roman was a problem the sport was scrambling to fix and yet here was Lukas making no effort to keep his distance. He hadn't made a statement condemning Roman's opinions either.

Was this a secret side of the champion? Did he hold similar beliefs to Roman? The two of them seemed friendly and Katherine wondered if this was a case of 'birds of a feather.'

She stored the information away for a possible story. But right now, she needed to make her way to the press area.

Once she was miked up with her cameraman behind her, Katherine put on her brightest smile, speaking to as many drivers as she could, waiting for her moment to speak to the champion.

And then it was happening. Lukas Jäger was about to enter the pen.

Almost in slow motion, she saw him walk towards her, his manager by his side, her anticipation ramping up. *This* was what she had worked so hard for. It was only the second day of the season opener, but she had so many questions for Lukas.

She never took her eyes off him. She couldn't. He was magnetic. So she saw when he looked at her and his expression turned cold, his brows drawing in a frown. The antithesis to how broadly he had smiled with Roman. She'd wondered if they held similar beliefs and Katherine felt like she was getting her answer.

She saw him mutter something to his manager and attempt to turn away, but almost instantly her producer was there, and she held her breath hoping he was trying to convince Lukas to give her a moment. Ultimately, they all wanted great footage for VelociTV.

Her hands wrung the microphone in a hard grip. It was the only sign of her anxiety, because she had to remain calm. Professional.

And then her heart sank.

Lukas walked away.

She watched his retreating back in utter disbelief. Never in all the years that she'd spent building her career had anyone refused to speak to her.

'Come with me.'

She startled at her producer's words, spoken right beside her. Uneasiness crept in her belly. What had Lukas said? She wanted to know what was happening but didn't dare speak as she followed him to the OB van.

'Everyone out,' he instructed, leaving Katherine alone with him. Then the door slid shut.

'We took you on because your lecturer vouched for you,' her producer said. 'Asked us to give you a chance.

But that means nothing if the drivers won't talk to you. You're no good to us if the *reigning champion* won't talk to you. You're done here. You're fired.'

'What?' Katherine cried out in disbelief, utterly shocked at the gross overreaction. 'You can't be serious. You can't just fire me! I've done my job. Who doesn't want to talk to me?'

'Lukas Jäger. He's competitive. He's always competitive, always going to be in the title hunt, which means we'll be speaking to him a lot. That makes you a liability. So yes, I can fire you.' He stated it as if Katherine's world imploding made no difference at all.

'Did Jäger actually tell you this?' Katherine demanded. She didn't understand why he would refuse to speak to her. Even if he was secretly against women in the sport, he had given interviews to women before. So why was he singling her out? Regardless of his reasons, his word shouldn't be enough to get her fired...but she suspected what was really going on.

'Or is this a convenient way for you to get rid of me? Don't think I haven't noticed how I'm the only woman reporting on Alpha One for VelociTV, or the way you all speak about the handful of female correspondents here. How you think the female strategists and engineers are somehow a liability. Just be honest!'

'First of all, yes, Lukas did say that to me. Second, you're no longer employed, so I don't care what you think. If you're going to be sensitive about it, go cry on some talk show. Give me back your pass. You're out of here.'

Katherine pulled off her lanyard, tossed it at him and threw open the van door. As she walked away, she tried to leash the utter devastation coursing through her. She'd gotten to live her dream so briefly before having it ripped from her, thanks to a misogynistic ass who happened to drive a car well.

That was fine, because this wasn't the end. She would find a way to show the world exactly who Lukas Jäger was.

CHAPTER ONE

THE CLACKING OF quick-fire typing on a mechanical keyboard died with an enthusiastic punch of the enter key.

'Done,' Katherine said to herself in the stillness of her home office. The sounds of London beyond the window returned in full force after the vacuous silence of moments before. The shelves of her office—lined with books and Lego plants, the only type she didn't kill—rematerialising as she came back from the place she disappeared into whenever she wrote an article. She was exceptionally proud of this one. A feature on Lukas Jäger, former Alpha One champion, currently without a drive for next year, and the man she hated more than anyone else.

Katherine was arguably one of the most popular journalists in the paddock. But it hadn't always been that way. She'd worked hard to become a key part of the presenter team of the official broadcaster, Aero TV. A position that had also won her her very own column on the network's sporting site.

It hadn't all been smooth sailing. Lukas Jäger was the reason for that. The reason she had been fired from her first position as an on-track correspondent for VelociTV, a smaller, but well-respected motorsport news network.

She still remembered that day three years ago when he'd

taken one look at her, turned around and walked away. She remembered the hope that had filled her when she saw her producer talk to him, thinking that maybe he would convince a media-shy driver to give her five minutes of his time. But that had never happened. That day her producer shattered her dream.

You're no good to us if the reigning champion won't talk to you. You're done here. You're fired.

Reporting on Alpha One had been Katherine's dream job, the sport a point of connection with her father. Something that was just for the two of them. Growing up, it was during those races that he'd noticed her, given her the attention she so craved but wouldn't ask for. Then because of an entitled chauvinist, that dream had almost died before it had even really begun. And she couldn't speak about her experience because she'd had to make sure another network or publication would hire her afterwards. One where a 'sensitive woman'—which the misogynists would undoubtedly call her—might be no more welcome than at VelociTV.

To protect her dream, she'd had to remain hireable.

Now here she was, writing a feature on the man whose name had constantly been churning in the rumour mill, whether he would secure a drive next season or if his career was over. And she hadn't held back.

Regardless of how Katherine felt about Lukas Jäger, she was a professional and, giving her article a once-over, she was satisfied with the balance of her reporting. She had presented the facts. Feeling more than a little pleased, she submitted her article, then took a look at the gold smartwatch on her wrist.

She smiled. 'I'll be early to dinner.' A dinner with her

family that she had been looking forward to all week. Well, it was more her parents that she had been keen to see.

She picked up her phone to send a message to the family chat to say she was on her way when she noticed her father's message.

Dinner is postponed. Paige got into a spot of trouble. Sorry. Love you, Kittykat.

'Of course,' Kat breathed. Her high from moments before dulled into the ever-familiar disappointment that came attached to mentions of her sister. Her twin sister. People often thought twins had to be close. That they would have to be alike and have a near telepathic connection, but that had never been the case with them. Where Katherine had succeeded, Paige had languished. When Katherine had chosen the path of academics and responsibility, Paige had chosen to party and move in the wrong crowd. And yet Paige was the one doted on by Christopher, their big brother. Paige was the fun one Nicholas—her younger brother that Katherine had helped raise—wanted to spend time with. Her parents had focussed most of their time on her siblings, especially Paige, because they needed it more than her.

Katherine was used to this. It wasn't a big deal, she always had work to do.

And as if the universe had heard her thoughts, the phone in her hand began to ring, flashing her producer's name.

'Hi, Robert,' she greeted.

'Kat, I need you to pack.'

'Okay. Should I come by the office?' Because of course there would be a meeting—an urgent one, by the sounds of it. And since her dinner plans had fallen through, there was no reason she couldn't drop everything and rush over before Robert had even uttered a summons. She glanced at her watch. 'I can be there in twenty minutes.'

'Good. Bring everything with you. You'll be flying out straight after.'

Well, there went dinner, but if Katherine was honest with herself, she would much rather work than sit at a table where she was reminded how different she was from her siblings. How she would never relate to them like they did with each other. If she was working, it would mean that she was being responsible. Ensuring that she was successful. Being the daughter her parents never had to worry about. The one who would one day take care of them in their old age because her siblings wouldn't be able to. Take care of Paige, the free spirit—a nice way of saying 'selfish and irresponsible.' Katherine had to. Her parents would never be able to retire, never be able to relax if there wasn't a safety net for Paige. They would always be run ragged.

At least, thanks to Paige, Katherine wouldn't have to run out on dinner, leaving behind a father who was proud of his Alpha One journalist daughter and a mother who was disappointed that Katherine wouldn't settle down to a quiet life of marriage and children. Bear the grandchildren she so desperately wanted that Katherine had no interest in. They had their hands full tonight.

'What's the rush? What am I covering?' Katherine asked, her curiosity well and truly piqued at the urgency. The season was over. Teams were on winter break. News was less urgent right now. Well, apart from the fact that a couple teams hadn't confirmed their driver line-up for next season yet. It was unheard of for them to wait quite so long but she had a sneaking suspicion that Lukas was at least a part of the reason why.

'Lukas Jäger's publicity stunt.'

She let out a noise of frustration. 'Robert... Anyone but Lukas.'

'I don't care, Kat. You will be there interviewing him,' her producer said firmly. 'It's a closed track, he'll be driving, you'll be asking questions.'

The very last thing she wanted was to be stuck in a car with him for hours on end.

'Viewers love seeing you two together and we're going to leverage that.'

She knew what the viewers thought. It was in the comments of every social media post that showed them together.

Wouldn't it be amazing if Lukas and Katherine dated?

There's something between Lukas and Katherine. I guarantee it.

#lukat for life!

There absolutely was something between her and Lukas: mutual hatred.

'I have no choice, do I?'

'None.'

You're doing this for your career. You need to be a success. You're not going to end up like Mum.

'Fine,' she replied. 'Where am I going?'

'Please tell me you're joking.' Lukas Jäger stared his manager down. 'I'm not going to Lapland with Katherine Ward, Dominic. Anyone but her.'

'Tough.'

Lukas let out a growl of frustration and walked away from his friend. The man who had managed his career from the moment he graduated from karting at fourteen and was ready to step into the feeder series. Now at thirty-three, he'd known Dominic for two decades, trusted him, and yet couldn't remember a time when he'd been more annoyed with the man than he was right now.

He stepped out onto the terrace of his Carré d'Or penthouse apartment looking out at Monaco, the bite of the chilly December air on his skin a welcome distraction.

Lukas didn't want to be anywhere near Katherine. He had worked so hard, his family had sacrificed so much for him to achieve this life. To be an Alpha One world champion. And he had done it not once, but thrice. But that didn't matter to Katherine. She'd taken every opportunity to cast doubt on his talent, on his character, on his commitment. So much so that he could see how it affected the way people treated him. Affected how many offers he received from teams, because it cast doubt on his talent... his ability to race in the future. When he'd lost his seat at the team, she'd gone out of her way to promote the driver who had taken his place. It had massively impacted the way the public viewed the change.

Footsteps sounded behind him but he didn't turn to look at Dominic. Instead, he folded his fingers around the metal railing that wrapped all the way around his three-storey apartment.

'You know how I feel about her,' Lukas said, eyes fixed on the steel-coloured water.

'I do, but, Lukas, this has been a bad season...'

'You—'

'It was a bad season because you didn't win the championship. Yes, we both know the car was a big reason for that,' Dominic said, cutting him off and coming to stand beside him. 'The second half of the season did a lot of damage. You had no pace in that car to mount any kind of challenge, and I know what it took for you to drag it to the podium. But regardless of the reason, you lost your drive. You need some good PR.'

'She's the reason I need good PR, Dom.' Lukas turned to face his manager. 'The shit she's been saying about Easton Rivers is exactly why no one cares how unfair it was that I lost my seat.'

'I get that, Lukas,' Dominic said patiently. 'But the things she says are true. Easton Rivers won his junior championship, he showed pace in his tests...'

'None of that matters!' Lukas raged. 'He's Thomas Dudek's driver. Dudek created a seat in the team he runs for the driver he manages! By dumping me!'

'I know, Lukas.'

'Plus, Easton comes with money. Dudek didn't have to give him my seat. Easton could have bought one! He could use all that sponsorship money for a back-marker team like Brock Racing who would gladly paste the name of his backers on their car. Those teams are uncompetitive, he could make a difference there and pay his dues. And what about the fact that we were promised a contract renewal? I met with Dudek, he assured me that there was no truth to Katherine's reports about Rivers taking my place. That it was all rumours.' Lukas paced like a caged animal.

'I had a similar conversation with him,' Dominic agreed.

'And we have no recourse? You know there is only one reason he waited until all the top teams' seats were filled before he announced Rivers as his driver.'

'I know, Lukas. You're right. He did it so that you wouldn't have a competitive seat. He knows that you would take another team to a driver's and possibly a constructor's title. I know it hurts that after all these years with the team he made you think he was announcing a renewal but announced Rivers instead. I *know*, Lukas. But we have to face reality. Your now former teammate, Will, is young and recently signed. They would never get rid of him. Not after one season and not with him being an academy driver. Not even with you finishing second and him eighth. And Rivers is in the other seat. Nothing will change that, so we need to look at alternatives. Negotiations will be difficult because you do have a "first driver" stipulation for any contract we pursue.'

Lukas slumped against the gold Art Deco porch post that served no other purpose than being decorative. 'Have I told you how much I love it when you're blunt?'

Dominic chuckled sympathetically. 'I know it isn't fair, but we need to work on what we can change. We can't undo anything that happened this year, but maybe we can salvage next year and get you something worthwhile and lucrative.'

Lucrative.

When Lukas had been a child racing around the local go-kart track in the foothills of the Ybbstal Alps of Austria in a kart his father built, with tyres cast off from rich parents looking to get rid of them, money had been the farthest thing from his mind. It had all been about the dream: to make it to Alpha One. Now so much of the negotiation revolved around money, but he would happily take a cut in earnings if it put him in a *competitive* seat. He didn't want to be at the back of the grid. He wanted to drive...and win.

He owed his father that much. Especially after he'd cost his father his marriage. A comfortable life. A stress-free life.

Would his father be disappointed in him after this nightmare of a year?

He couldn't know. Couldn't contact the dead. All Lukas

could do was make every choice that would take him back to the sharp end of the grid.

'Whether you like it or not,' Dom went on, 'Katherine is loved by the fans, so you need to work with her. Leverage the public's opinion of the two of you.'

Lukas scoffed. 'You mean play into the idiotic fantasy of the two of us being a couple? Hell will freeze over first.'

Dominic sighed.

'Dom, you know how I feel about the media. The off-season allows me my space. My privacy. But more importantly, I don't want to be around the woman who championed the driver who took my seat. If you recall, it was Katherine who said that it was a "no-brainer" to replace me with Easton. She questioned whether other teams like Brock Racing would actually consider taking on me, a driver at the end of his career. Do you remember that?'

'I do, but think about how it will appear if the person who is so against you is in a car appearing to have a good time with you. Asking you questions to keep the world thinking about you.'

Lukas laughed as he ran a hand through his hair. He understood exactly what Dominic had done. 'You asked for her to do this, didn't you?'

His friend and manager simply smiled. 'You need to keep in the public eye to keep your prospects alive. If the teams that haven't yet finalised their line-up for next year don't consider you, you will be without a drive. And then your only option is retirement. All the reserve driver roles are taken. Every single one of them is younger than you. Even if we do manage to wrangle up some sort of additional driver position, are you going to be happy doing publicity stunts and sim work?'

'No,' Lukas admitted. But those weren't his only options. There was another. One he hadn't mentioned to Dominic or anyone because he didn't want to consider it at all.

A new team would be entering the sport next season. A small team that had approached Lukas to lead them. It would make him the youngest team principal in the sport's history. The car had less than no chance of winning in their first season, let alone scoring points, but it would be an opportunity to grow the organization and grow as a leader with it.

Lukas Jäger: boss of an Alpha One team. He couldn't picture it. Or rather, he didn't want to picture being in charge of the day-to-day running of a team. Overseeing the team and car's performance from an office and the pitwall. Lukas didn't want that. Didn't want to consider it even for a moment because it meant his career as a driver would undeniably be over. There would be no way back into the cockpit.

No way to repay his father for all the sacrifices.

'Fine. I'll go to Finland, but I have conditions.'

'I knew you would. Let's hear it.'

Lukas fought a smile at how well Dominic knew him. 'It's obvious we'll be forced to stay there at least overnight, so I want my accommodation away from Aero.'

'Fair enough. What else?'

'Katherine Ward only has access to me while we're shooting.' There was absolutely no way he was going to make it easier for her to gather ammunition on him to further spit her vitriol.

CHAPTER TWO

LUKAS STOOD AT the large wooden door of his luxury cabin, pulling up the zip of his thick insulated jacket, then buttoning up the fabric flap that covered the zipper. His feet were already in a pair of black snow-boots. Knowing how cold it could get out there, he made sure to prepare for it.

He placed his hand on the door-handle and inhaled deeply. This publicity stunt was the last thing in the world he wanted to do but here he was. There was no turning back now.

Lukas yanked open the door and stared at the wonderland that was Lapland. There were tall pine trees everywhere. Their barks taking on a greyish hue from the snow caught on every bump and knot. They were topped in white, like nature's very own dusting of powdered sugar. It was truly beautiful and, were it not for the events planned for that day, Lukas would quite happily have gone snowmobiling or sledding or snowshoeing and then returned to sit at the large window with the fire roaring and something warm clutched in his hands.

But that peaceful fantasy would never happen whilst he was forced to be around Katherine.

Lukas stepped out and shut the door behind him. There was a driver waiting in a dark four-wheel drive SUV. The most efficient way to trek across the snow was the most efficient way to get anywhere: in something with an engine. And at least that made Lukas smile.

'Good morning, Mr Jäger.' The driver, who'd donned a thick black jacket with bright splashes of colour, greeted Lukas as he climbed into the front passenger seat.

He was far too cheerful. Especially when Lukas was dreading the next few hours.

Put on your media face, Dominic had begged when Lukas Zoom called him earlier.

'Morning,' Lukas grunted. Thankfully the driver caught the hint and said nothing more. Lukas needed to hold on to all of his finite patience if he was to make it through filming with Katherine.

Katherine.

The very thought of her name was like a poker in his frontal lobe. He tried to focus on why he was doing this. To save his career. To make his father's sacrifices worth something. To get back in an Alpha One car. He never felt so alive as he did when he blasted down the pit straight in his single-seater, at 350 kilometres an hour. The world a blur. A tunnel focussed on one point: turn one. When he got his braking just right and nailed that first apex—he always knew at that point if it was going to be a good lap or not. And then he would put those laps in. Time after time after time.

He never felt more alive, but he also never felt closer to his father. He could feel his father's pride then, and Lukas could forget for a moment that he was the reason his mother left.

He needed to race. It gave his life meaning, so he would do this. He would grin when he had to, and bear this invasion.

As they approached, Lukas could make out part of a track that had been carved and smoothed in the snow. The closer they got, the more he could see. A simple course that weaved through the trees and back again with a section over the frozen lake.

The SUV came to a stop near a two-door sports car. One that had no affiliation with any of the Alpha One teams on track. So, unlike all the other stunts he had done in his career where the cars had always been linked to his team. Another reminder that Lukas was a driver without a tether. That he needed the day to go well.

The car was bright red. Easily filmed. Dynamic in the monochrome environment. There were cameras fixed to the outside of it in several places, plus three that he could see on the inside. He and Katherine would be on show. Nowhere to hide. He couldn't allow a single expression to give away his reluctance to be there.

He stepped out of the vehicle and noticed the team of people like little black specks on a white canvas. Equipment everywhere even though he knew they would be invisible in the end result. Every one of these people would be ghosts, and all anyone would see would be him and Katherine.

Then would come the posts that set his teeth on edge. Lukat. He hated the portmanteau. The absurdity of the very idea.

'This way, Mr Jäger,' the man who had driven him said.

'It's Lukas,' he replied, looking at the profile of the corners of their track as they walked together. At least that would be fun.

'Lukas!' He heard his name being called as they reached a large tent from which the snow track was no longer visible. And, in what felt like a flash, he was surrounded by people. One attacked him with makeup while another affixed a mic to his clothes while a third and fourth briefed him on what he would be doing. For most people this would be too much, but he wasn't most people. He heard and understood every word being said, felt every swipe of the sponge on his face, was aware of exactly where the mic was clipped and the wire run. And still he felt the air change. Felt her very presence before he even saw her, and despite hating her for the things she'd written about him, for playing a part in him losing his seat, Lukas turned to find the burning blue eyes of Katherine Ward staring back at him. Her red hair, perfectly styled to look effortlessly elegant, hung over her right shoulder. Her skin was like porcelain. And her plump lips, the bottom a little fuller than top, pressed together in a thin line.

A prickle travelled under Lukas's skin but he kept looking. Looking at her jacket that appeared warm but Lukas knew it wasn't. A fashionable piece of apparel designed to look good in pictures and videos. He had seen tourists come to his town, the chilliest in Austria, dressed as she was, ill-equipped for the intense cold of the mountains which attracted thousands each year, only for them to run into trouble and rush back into town or worse, have emergency services rush out to them. The longer he looked at the jacket the more irritated he became, and he knew it was settling into his expression. An expression that was mirrored on hers.

'We'll give you two a moment while we get ready,' the director said. 'We'll start shooting with you both putting your helmets on. We only really have about two hours of good light to get everything done so we need to hustle.'

'Understood,' Katherine replied, but Lukas said nothing. All he did was cross his arms over his chest.

* * *

Katherine had watched Lukas keenly as she had approached. He stood maybe two inches shy of six feet. Though hidden in a thick jacket, his body was still clearly in peak physical shape. Light brown hair that was so very nearly blond crowned a head that sat on a thick, muscular neck. This man was an elite athlete. A weapon crafted to withstand the immense forces of an Alpha One race car, and the off-season hadn't dulled him at all. And when she saw him, she fought a shiver. A knot in her stomach that formed whenever he was close.

You're no good to us if the reigning champion won't talk to you. You're done here.

This man had been the reason she was fired and yet he had the audacity to look at her as if *she* was some irritation. The gall!

'Nice of you to join us,' she sniped.

'I'm perfectly on time,' he said, adjusting the cuff of his jacket. It was thick and bulky. Not in any way sexy. Not chosen for the cameras. He looked utterly comfortable in it. Warm. Yet she had to fight off shivers as the wind bit through her jacket. Had to look impeccable for the cameras.

Are you some incredible beauty? Because you're not getting on camera if you aren't.

Words from her university lecturer, the man who had given her the incredible reference that led to her job at VelociTV, who had promised to never hide the unspoken side of being a media personality. His words had made her go home and look at herself in the mirror, and make an effort to look good every moment of every day. Because it didn't matter how much she knew, no one would give her the time of day if she wasn't also a pretty face. If she didn't have a beach-ready body throughout the year.

So seeing Lukas's warm jacket turned that knot in her stomach into a ball of fire.

'And yet I could find it in me to get here a few minutes early.'

'That's your job, not mine.' His grey eyes looked almost bored. He hadn't uncrossed his arms. Had barely spoken to the people around him. Katherine had to be 'on' at all times. Keep that bubbly, media personality up around everyone she worked with. It was exhausting. But men like Lukas…they got to be grouchy and ill-tempered, and people would find an excuse for his behaviour. She hated it.

Hated him.

'And what is your job, Lukas? Certainly not racing. Not currently, at least.' She took great pleasure in the way his eyes narrowed. In the frown on his face. Her pulse galloped as he stalked towards her, knowing she had gotten under his skin. But nothing she said could even remotely make up for the fact that he had gotten her fired. That he had nearly destroyed her and her father's dream.

'You must be enjoying this immensely,' he said through his teeth in his hard accent. 'This is exactly what you wanted. It's right there in your little articles. "Lukas Jäger Is Done." Well, I'm not.' He stood right in front of her, making her look up into the grey eyes that looked so at home in the icy surroundings.

'I report the truth, Lukas. If you don't like it, maybe you need to look at yourself for a solution.'

'Kat!'

Whatever Lukas was about to say died as they both looked at one of the production assistants, who waved her over. She didn't bother excusing herself from him. She owed him no politeness. She simply walked away.

But she felt him follow behind. She fought off another shiver.

'Stupid jacket,' she mumbled.

'We're ready to go,' the production assistant informed her. Soon a transmitter that her lavalier mic plugged into was hidden in her clothes, sound checks were done and they were making their way to the track. Another production assistant was waiting for her and Lukas there, holding their helmets.

'Given how slow you've been this year, you should be able to manage the course easily enough. Though your edge seems to be pretty dead at this point, so we could end up in a snowbank.' Was antagonising the man who was about to drive her in a high-powered car on ice a wise move? Probably not, but Katherine had a need to make him as irritated as his presence made her even if she knew deep down that he wasn't slow. That he was as competitive as he had always been.

'You would love that, wouldn't you?' Lukas replied, snatching the helmet out of the hands of the innocent bystander, who was undeserving of his bad mood. 'After all, vultures are only happy when there's death.'

'How dare you?'

'You wanted me to face truths, maybe you should heed your own advice.' He rounded the car, helmet in hand. Katherine could feel the burn in her cheeks, but had to force the outrage down because there was a countdown in her ear. And just like that she plastered a smile on her face.

She noticed Lukas staring at her. Shaking his head in disgust. Whatever. She was here to do a job, and she would be the professional.

She placed the helmet on her head, but couldn't get the belt fastened. It wasn't a side release buckle clip as she had been expecting but rather a double D-ring and without a mirror she just couldn't figure it out with her gloved hands. She could bend down to have a look in the side mirror of the car but that would be a terrible angle and with so little good light, every frame had to be perfect.

And that's when she felt a hand on her shoulder. As if it burned straight through her jacket and singed her skin. She looked up to find Lukas, who grit his teeth before his lips relaxed into a small smile.

'It took me a while to get the hang of these while wearing gloves,' he said.

He was helping her. Why? 'It takes some practice,' she heard herself say.

He smirked. 'And I have plenty.' He reached past her to open the door, allowing her to catch a whiff of his cologne. It made her feel warm. Conjured images of a fireplace and a goblet of cognac.

She grinned, remembering they were on camera and every movement was being recorded. 'What a gentleman.'

'I hope you don't have a weak heart,' he teased when he climbed into the driver's side.

'Oh, don't you worry. It's perfectly steady.' That was a lie. It was pounding. Whether from anger or the shock of his one-eighty, her heart was anything but steady.

'We'll see about that.' There was a twinkle in his eye just as he started the car that roared to life. 'Ready?'

She checked her seat belts and nodded, ignoring how his presence filled the space. 'Let's do this!'

The engine screamed as he took off in the snow. The back end of the car fishtailed with the lack of traction and Lukas grinned. Katherine did too. She couldn't help it. His excitement was contagious but it wasn't just that, this right here was what she dreamed of as a child. Being in a fast car with an Alpha One driver in the most unimaginable places and she whooped in delight as they drifted around a corner, a tree flashing by in a blur. And she heard Lukas chuckle. A deep rumble that seemed to come straight from his chest.

'Okay, Lukas, you still need to answer these questions,' she said for the cameras.

'Not if you can't read them.'

He dropped a gear and floored the gas, nearly sending them into a spin that he controlled effortlessly, even though it nearly sent her papers flying. He laughed harder than she had ever heard before. But even with him trying to make her job difficult, she managed to ask all the questions she had prepared and some that she thought of in the moment, and when the car came to a stop where they had started, the director yelled 'Cut!'

'That was fantastic! You two were great!'

'Yeah,' the production assistant agreed. 'Viewers are going to *love* this, Kat.'

Once she and Lukas stepped out, whatever truce they had found within the confines of the car was obliterated. The scowl was back on his face.

'We just need to do one more take of the ice section and then take it from there,' the director said.

'You have to be kidding,' Lukas groused. 'Why?'

'We have great footage of you and Kat in the car but had some technical difficulties with one of the exterior cameras, so we're just swapping that out and we'll be good to go. You two can get back in the car in the meantime.'

The man walked away and Katherine retrieved her helmet from the assistant, who still stood close by.

'This is ridiculous,' Lukas muttered, drumming his fingers on the roof of the car.

This man was so aggravating. 'You know this entire stunt benefits you, Lukas. You could stand to be more gracious about it.' She jammed the helmet on her head and let the assistant do up the straps this time. 'I have it so much worse. I have to be stuck in that car with you, but you don't see *me* complaining.'

'Oh please,' Lukas snapped. 'What do you have to complain about? Your face is on TV. You'll get enough content from this to fuel more of your distorted reports.'

'My reports aren't distorted. No one else has a problem with them, it's only you! And you know what?' She stepped away from the assistant and rounded on Lukas, the car between them. 'It's entirely your own fault. *You* didn't win the championship. *You* are difficult to work with. There's plenty of footage proving you could be nice if you wanted to be, but you don't.'

Which was why Katherine was proud of the article she had written. After it came out, the world would question the kind of person Lukas really was. Because if they could see him now, there was no doubt in her mind that others would question his authenticity too. 'This is who you are. A grouchy, unfriendly, snob. Those nice things you do for fans, it's a farce. You're a two-faced hypocrite and it's my job to report on the truth.'

A two-faced hypocrite?

That was what Lukas got for trying. He hated being in front of the cameras. Inviting people into his life. Allowing strangers to attempt to read him. Performing with a smile when his skin crawled at the idea of being in the media.

Lukas didn't even really have social media. He had profiles that his publicist managed. He gave them a few hours of his time to create content and he never had to document his private life for anyone.

But here he was, in his time off. Time that he usually used to decompress from life in the fast lane. When he could relax and breathe and put the hyper-competitive side of him away. When he made time for his mother, just in case, even though he knew she wouldn't call. Wouldn't ask him to visit her in Salzburg.

Right now Lukas couldn't do any of those things. His need to find a drive forced him to be in situations like these, where he had to spend time with the media he so detested.

They were always so unfair to him, but he just had to bear it. And yet Katherine had the audacity to call him a hypocrite? Say *he* was the one who wasn't gracious?

'What would you know about the truth?' he spat and got in the car before she had a chance to respond. When they called 'action' again, he poured his frustration into the car. Felt the very instant the front tyre went from contact with compacted snow to ice. When the car began to slide. Heard Katherine squeal. In delight. In panic. He didn't care. She was far away to him now, because in the moment he was a young boy in a kart his father had built with used, cast-off tyres—the only tyres they could afford—on a small icy track close to home.

And he was free. Ice, snow, a fine spray of water flew out from beneath his tyres and this was love. This was the feeling he chased. In that moment, he could have almost sworn that he saw his father standing on the side, cheering as no one else ever did. He couldn't abandon this feeling to be a team principal. Couldn't turn his back on the memories of his father. He felt Florian's presence when he drove.

Lukas could hear Katherine talk. Was certain he was answering her. If it wasn't for the fact they had to wrap up filming, he would have happily spent the rest of the day out on this frozen lake.

'That was incredible!' was the first thing Lukas heard when he got out of the car. 'This segment is going to be amazing.'

It probably would be, but would it be enough to create more of a buzz around him to get his phone ringing?

'We have a little bit of good light left so we were thinking of shooting one more segment. Get some action shots. Those would be great for promos. Maybe Kat can drive,' the director said.

That caught Lukas's attention. 'What?'

'There's a storm coming later so if we could get extra footage, it would be great.'

'I love the idea!' Katherine beamed.

Of course she did.

'Absolutely not,' Lukas said in a voice he rarely used. 'I'm not trusting her to drive this—' he patted the car '—out there. I'm not risking an injury.' He counted down the seconds to Katherine's explosion in his head. It was barely two.

'Excuse me!' Katherine very nearly shouted.

'Um…yes…well,' the field producer said, 'it would still be good to get those extra shots, so you two can head over to the tent for some touch-ups and a warm drink. We'll call for you when we're ready.' He and the director walked away, leaving Lukas and Katherine to head for the tent set beyond the tree-line, well away from where they filmed.

'You're such a misogynist!' Katherine accused as soon as they were away from the rest of the team. No one around to see them eviscerate each other. 'Just because

I'm a woman you assume that I'll be a bad driver. God!' She was quite literally red in the face.

Lukas was well and truly tired of how lowly Katherine thought of him.

'It's not because you're a woman. It's because you're you. I don't trust *you*.' He wouldn't trust anyone from this crew in those conditions. Things very easily went from fun to dangerous on a track, never mind a frozen lake and snowy landscape where the trees beckoned.

Lukas sought thrills, but he was never reckless.

'I cannot be around you for one minute longer, Lukas Jäger,' Katherine huffed. She turned around and stormed off.

'Where are you going? That's not where the tent is,' Lukas called.

'Away from you!' she yelled back.

Fine. Let her go off. She wasn't his concern.

CHAPTER THREE

KATHERINE DISAPPEARED FROM VIEW.

Lukas just wanted to be done with the day. Time alone would be welcome, but Katherine having walked away left him feeling uneasy.

He felt the direction of the wind change. Knew there was a storm incoming that night. They should all be away from there by the time it happened but then he thought of that ridiculous jacket Katherine was wearing and cursed. She should be safe…but the mountains he'd grown up around should have been safe too, and he still remembered careless tourists perishing while trying to explore.

They weren't in Austria now. Nor were they in London. Storming off was a stupid thing for Katherine to do and try as he might, Lukas's conscience wouldn't let him leave without knowing she was okay.

He cursed once more for good measure and walked in the direction that Katherine had gone, then stopped. A rope, coiled loosely, sat in the snow. Someone from the production team must have dropped it there with the intention of fetching it later. Instinct from living so close to the mountains took over and he picked it up, draping it over his shoulder, then set off to look for the woman he hated more than anyone else.

* * *

'Katherine!' he called, after walking for ages and seeing no sign of her. The wind had picked up speed and glancing overhead, he saw that dark, ominous clouds had gathered. The storm was coming in much faster than they had anticipated and by the looks of it, would be worse too.

'Katherine!' he called again. Louder. He needed to find her soon because they wouldn't have much time to find shelter. Then he thought, what if she wasn't answering because it was him who was calling? He could see her being that petty. Everyone else on the shoot had called her 'Kat.' Even in the paddock hardly anyone used her full name. But Lukas did. He always did.

So as he walked a little farther, he shouted 'Kat!' as loud as he could manage.

'I'm here!' came a soft, strained response and his body simultaneously sagged in relief and went on high alert.

'I'm coming! Keep talking!'

'I'm in a crevasse. I fell.'

Lukas's body went cold. Those were the last words he wanted to hear. He ran in the direction of her voice, sliding to a stop as snow sprayed over the edge of a narrow gap like a powdery waterfall.

Lukas lay on his stomach, flattening himself on the snow and crawling slowly to the edge. Peering in, he saw Katherine on a ledge.

'Lu-Lu-Lukas?' she could barely get his name out for how badly she was shivering. Her skin was bright red. The edges of her lips where she had bitten off her lipstick were starting to turn slightly blue. He needed to get her out now.

'Are you hurt?'

'I hurt my ankle when I fell but otherwise, I'm okay.'

That was a relief to hear. 'Hang on, I'll get you out.'

Lukas looked around. There were no trees where they had come. Nothing but snow in all directions. This was less than ideal. He would have to be the anchor to pull Katherine up. He couldn't afford for anything to go wrong. How ironic it was that he hadn't wanted Katherine to drive, because he didn't trust her in a car on a safe track, and yet now, if anything went wrong it could be the end of them both.

Lukas grabbed the rope, tying a figure eight knot like his father had taught him, ensuring the loop at the end was big enough to go around Katherine, and made his way back to the edge.

'Put the loop around you,' he instructed as he lowered the rope down. Once it was around her torso and her shoulders free, he gave her the next set of instructions. 'Hold on to the rope tightly. Don't try to climb it, I will pull you up. Got it?'

Katherine nodded.

'Yes or no. I need to know you understand.'

'Yes,' she said, through chattering teeth.

Once he was satisfied that she was following his instructions, he moved away from the edge lest he fall too, and pulled. One hand over the other. The rope burned his palms but he didn't care. He was singularly focussed. He pulled, and kept pulling until he saw hands and the top of a jacket hood emerge. Lukas, keeping tension with one hand, lunged with his other and grabbed ahold of Katherine's forearm, pulling her out of the crevasse and placing her safely on the snowy ground.

'Th-th-thank y-y-you,' she stuttered through chattering teeth. Lukas knew he had to get her warm immediately.

He ignored her thanks. Instead he looked her over for any signs of injury. Anything that could complicate their next mission: finding refuge from the storm. The wind was already whipping around them.

'Can you stand?' he asked as he helped her to her feet.

'I think so,' Katherine replied but struggled to keep her balance as she hobbled two steps in the snow. The wind was picking up the snow on the surface and curling it around them. They didn't have time to hobble. And with her shaking so badly, progress would be slow. Lukas had only one choice. He placed his arms around her back and under her knees, then lifted her against his chest. His body came to life as if he'd been struck with a bolt of electricity the moment he held her to him. He ignored the feeling, not willing to analyse it when there were more important things at hand.

Her body, racked by shivers, trembled in his arms and he cursed her ridiculous jacket. There was nothing he could do about it now except fight his way through the storm that was already upon them. And as hard as it was to struggle through the wind and snow that was stinging his face, it was nowhere close to as bad as it would get.

Lukas noticed Katherine's eyes starting to droop.

'Don't sleep,' he instructed.

'I'm so tired,' she slurred.

That wasn't good.

'Talk to me.' He needed to keep her awake.

'About what?' Snowflakes landed on her lashes and he had to fight the urge to brush them away. He had to keep walking. The cabins weren't far from the track. He just had to keep going and he would get them there.

'Eyes open,' he commanded, and she obeyed. Blue irises peered at him through half-closed lids. His heart rate sped up, which was ridiculous. He wasn't exerting himself enough for it to do so this frantically. 'Anything.'

'I like polar bears.'

'There are no polars bears here.'

'That's a shame.'

There were no polar bears but there were trees. Trees he recognised and as Lukas made his way through them, he saw the cabins come into view.

Cabins that were dark even though the vehicles were out front. It made sense for his cabin, there was no one there, but not the other.

Lukas climbed up the front steps to the small porch that was already covered in a layer of snow and, balancing Katherine's body against his, managed to open the door. When he stepped inside, he saw that nothing had been packed up. Items that belonged to the crew lay on several surfaces but there was no fire in the fireplace. No lights switched on.

'Hello?' Lukas called but no answer returned.

The crew were gone.

They were alone.

When they realised how close the storm was, they would have likely been airlifted out. And Lukas was annoyed. Annoyed that the production team had been operating on outdated information. Annoyed that Katherine had stormed off because no one had seen them walk away. The evacuation would likely have been chaotic. Lukas was certain both teams would have just assumed that he and Katherine were with the other. Their absence would only have been noticed once everyone was together. And now, with no one on the team having any idea where they could be, they would be deemed missing.

No one would come looking for them in a blizzard. No rescue would risk more lives for the chance of finding them.

'I hope you're happy now,' he grumbled but Katherine's response was unintelligible. Her skin getting a bluish tinge.

'Dammit!' He placed Katherine gently on one of the couches and raced to the closest room where he ripped a thick duvet from the bed and returned to her. 'I need to get you out of these clothes.' A sentence he never thought he'd say.

The snow had dampened them, making them a hazard. He removed her jacket first, flinging it across the room as if it was to blame for all that had befallen them. He took off her shoes then stripped off her socks, blouse, jeans and lastly her thermals, exposing her fair skin. Her toned body. Soft dips and peaks of her abdominals that she obviously worked hard for. Lukas had never thought he would ever be in this position: exposing Katherine like this. Once maybe, for a fleeting moment when he first saw her in the paddock and was struck by her absolute beauty. But he hadn't spoken to her. He hadn't wanted to. He hadn't wanted to be attracted to someone he would never allow in his life. Not when he was already in a vulnerable place. And now here he was, wanting to run the backs of his fingers down her face, along her body.

But he couldn't do that. He wouldn't. Not when they hated each other so much. Not when he knew she wouldn't want him to touch her at all if they weren't in this emergency. This want was a physical reaction and he was able to control his body. So he checked that her underwear was dry and when he was satisfied that it was, he wrapped her in the duvet.

He cradled her face, forcing her to look at him. 'I need you to stay awake. Can you do that for me?'

She nodded her head yes, then shook her head no.

'Try.'

He left her on the couch and went to the fireplace. Thankfully there were dry logs stacked beside it and he quickly got a roaring flame burning.

'That should do it.' He stood and stripped his own clothes, then picked up Katherine and sat with her on the rug in front of the fire with his back against the sofa. Her skin scalded his despite how cold she was. And with tense muscles, he wrapped the duvet around them both.

'You're freezing,' he said, wrapping his warm legs around her cold ones and rubbing her chest, trying his best to get warmth into her. But the contact of her skin on his made him tingle everywhere they touched. He ignored it. It was just the temperature difference that made him feel that way. Nothing more. She was the reason they were in this situation at all but when he looked down at her half-open eyes that looked like they were barely seeing anything, some of that anger melted away. He just needed her to warm up. To get her fire back.

Why do you care?

Lukas had no answer. All he knew was that he needed her to be okay. That he would only feel relief once she was bickering with him again. He didn't want to recognise how good he felt having her in his arms. This embrace, while it wracked him with worry, also calmed him. His mind had been going a million miles an hour since his contract hadn't been renewed, but right now, he didn't think about how he had been wronged. All he thought about was Katherine.

He could feel her slowly warming up, so it was probably safe to leave her long enough to make her a hot tea.

'Are you still with me?' he asked softly over her shoulder.

'Hmm' was all the reply he got.

'Can you sit here by yourself for a bit?' He tried to push off the warm rug, but Katherine's weak grip tightened around his wrist.

'No. Please don't go.'

Lukas could feel the shock on his face. Here was the woman who hated him asking him to stay. That look of vulnerability on her face, lit only by the fire in the dark cabin, was difficult to bear.

'I'm just going to get you some tea.'

'Stay with me,' she begged. 'Please.'

And against his better judgement, he sat back down, adjusting both their bodies so they were lying on the rug. Warm.

'I'm not going anywhere,' he promised, knowing how temporary a promise it was because as soon as she was back to normal, as soon as it was safe, he would very definitely go back to keeping his distance from her. This reporter who—no matter how beautiful she was—was as unscrupulous as they came.

CHAPTER FOUR

WARMTH. TOO MUCH WARMTH. Katherine could feel heat radiating on her back. A heavy weight draped over her. A weaker heat warming her face. None of this made sense.

She forced her eyes open and as her sight cleared, saw the dying embers in a fireplace she had no recollection of settling before. That was obviously the source of the warmth on her face but couldn't be responsible for the heat on her back. And as the fog lifted from her brain, she felt the softness of a cushion under her head. The hard, unyielding muscle of a well-toned arm under her neck. Another arm over her torso.

Heart racing with confusion and apprehension, Katherine followed the line of the muscular arm to a bare, sculpted chest. She shut her eyes.

'Please, God, don't let it be who I think it is,' she prayed and when she opened her eyes, was met with the sleeping face of Lukas Jäger. She swore and tried to push away, but when she threw the thick duvet off herself, she saw that she was only in her underwear and clutched the covers to her chest.

'Calm down,' a sleepy voice said. She watched him roll to his feet, clad only in a pair of tight black boxer briefs.

'Please tell me we didn't,' she whispered tightly.

'Relax. I prefer my partners a lot less comatose.'

'What the hell happened last night?' She couldn't remember coming back to the cabin. Scrunching her eyes shut, she tried to piece her memory together. She'd stormed off after their argument and hadn't noticed the crack in the snow that gave way when she stepped on the edge of it. She'd twisted her ankle.

She shoved the covers off her foot to examine the injury, noting that the joint was only slightly swollen and nowhere near as tender as it had been.

'It's not sprained or broken. The muscle tenderness should go away in a day or two,' Lukas said. He was obviously watching her but she couldn't look at him. He had pulled her from the crevasse but her memories after that were foggy. She couldn't remember how they'd gotten back.

'Why am I almost naked? Where are my clothes? Where is everyone? Why are *you* here?'

'I'm here,' Lukas said lowly, 'because I'm the only one who came to find you. Because everyone else left before the storm hit. You're almost naked, Katherine, because if I hadn't removed your clothes, you would have developed hypothermia and I really didn't want your death on my conscience.'

'You removed my clothes? You looked at me?' The thought of being in that vulnerable position with Lukas of all people was horrifying.

'I'm an Alpha One racing driver. I think I am perfectly capable of removing your clothes without looking.' His nonchalance was triggering.

'Turn around,' she snapped and tossed off the duvet to go in search of her clothes. 'So you took off my wet clothes and planted me by a fire.' The thought of having spent the entire night in Lukas's arms made lava flow through her veins.

Why would the Fates send the man she hated the most to rescue her? Why would he stay with her? He never wanted to be around her. He would never have done this out of the goodness of his heart. The man who got her fired had no heart.

She shoved her legs into her thermals and then into the jeans that were nearby. Why did you stay?' She hastily put on her blouse but now that she was no longer under the covers with Lukas or close to the embers, her skin erupted in goose bumps. She needed her jacket but it was nowhere to be found.

She heard Lukas's mirthless laughter. 'So ungrateful to the one person who kept you alive,' he spat.

Katherine caught a glimpse of the jacket on the floor, finding it balled up. Obviously having been thrown. Evidence of Lukas's anger at having helped her. 'Because why would you? You do nothing without an ulterior motive. The only reason you're even here in Lapland is because doing publicity suited you. How does helping me suit you?' She turned around to find Lukas fully dressed. His eyes flashing as they raked over her jacket.

'It doesn't suit me,' he gritted out. 'But I'm not an animal who would leave someone to die as you seem to be insinuating.' He turned towards her, grey eyes offended. Angry. An icy fire burning in them. 'You try to turn the world against me...' A step towards her. '...insult me...' Another step. The air slowly being sucked out of the room. '...could not even bother to thank me for saving your life when it's your fault we're in this mess.' One more step. Why did he loom so large? 'Your fault the world will be thinking that we're missing. *I* am the reason we made it out of that storm. So push me away.' He was in front of her now. 'Slap me across the face for undressing you and tell me to leave you.' He crowded her against the wall. Katherine wasn't breathing. An electrical storm brewed in the space between them. 'But you can't, can you? Because I'm the only one here.'

He had a point, but she couldn't give in to him. She couldn't *not* fight him. She couldn't give him the benefit of the doubt. Not ever. 'No one asked you to be here and I didn't turn the world against you. I told the truth, Easton Rivers is the future of that team. You aren't.'

Lukas shook his head. Katherine could feel the passion of his hate burning in his gaze. 'You still can't say "Thank you for saving me, Lukas. Thank you for not letting me succumb to hypothermia and ending my miserable career that way."'

Maybe he was right about that one point, but she couldn't get her mouth to form around the words. So she said nothing.

Of course, she said nothing. Lukas expected nothing less. She couldn't show him gratitude and she couldn't be apologetic for what she had written even though she knew he was still fully capable of winning another championship.

He pushed off the wall, needing to get away from her. Needing space, but that was secondary to *their* most important need, which was surviving. So whether or not she thanked him, it made no difference to what he had to do.

'Get a fire going in the kitchen stove.' He forced himself to be calm. To push aside his anger and frustration. He had to clear head. 'I'm going to see if I can call for help.'

'You mean you haven't tried yet?' Katherine accused.

'No, and you should be glad of it because if I had, you'd

be dead or comatose.' How different she was now to the woman who had begged him not to leave her. He could throw that in her face. Tell her how she'd clung to him, but what good would that do?

Lukas left her standing in the open plan living area to search the cabin for anything he could use. If he could just get word out that they were safe, he could get ahead of any crazy stories that might spread through the media. He could get word to Dominic...and his mother. Would she be worried?

He went through each room. Opened every cupboard. Searched every drawer until he found the answer to his prayers. A handheld radio. Lukas turned the device on and the screen lit up in blue. The battery still held some charge. He was about to try calling for help on it, try every frequency he could, but he couldn't do so alone in that room. Katherine had a right to hear what he found as well. She also wouldn't believe him no matter what he reported, so he took it into the kitchen and sat at the table. The chair slightly scraping the wooden floor caught Katherine's attention and she approached the table that now had the radio and Lukas's cell phone side by side. He tapped his phone screen—the status bar read 'No service.' He'd known it would, but he had to see it again anyway.

'Have you tried it yet?' There was hope in her voice.

Lukas shook his head. 'I thought you would like to be present if I managed to get through to anyone. Understand, it's a long shot.'

Katherine nodded. Lukas picked up the radio, praying it would work, and tried calling out but all he got back was static. He tried a different frequency but it was the same. And another and another.

His stomach sank and he realised how hopeful he'd been

that it would work. Hope was dangerous in a situation like this. 'We just have to wait it out.'

He scrubbed a hand down his face. He had no idea how long the storm would last. It wasn't blowing as hard now as it had been the night before, but it was still impossible for anyone to be moving around in that weather, which meant he had no idea how long he would be stuck with Katherine. A woman so stubborn that she hadn't even started the fire in the stove. Certain she was just being difficult, he did it himself with gritted teeth.

'You need a better jacket and to drink something hot,' he said curtly as he closed the stove door. The flames beyond the glass licked the fresh logs, scorching the surfaces black.

'You may have assisted me last night, Lukas, and I am grateful, but *you* do not get to tell me what to do.' She crossed her arms over her chest, leaning against the kitchen table, refusing to look at the stove at all.

'What?' The nerve of this woman. He could have gone back to his own cabin. He would have been happier there but he'd stayed to make sure she was alright.

'You heard me. I'm a grown woman. I can take care of myself.'

Lukas threw the lighter that was in his hand on the table with loud clatter. 'You know what? Have at it. At least in my cabin I'll have some peace.' He stormed to the door. 'Good luck.' He didn't even bother looking back as he opened the door to howling wind and slammed it shut behind him.

CHAPTER FIVE

KATHERINE WATCHED HIM LEAVE. Heard the glass rattle from the force.

'Great!' she yelled at the closed door, relieved to see him go. Her chest rose and fell as if she had run a sprint. That was how Lukas affected her, how much he agitated her, and in his absence she could slowly calm down. But in the wake of his leaving, it had grown quiet.

'I don't need him,' she said to herself. 'I've been on my own for years.'

She could hear her every breath. Feel the chill settling on her skin once more.

'I need to get warmer.' The kitchen stove had already begun warming the cabin but it wasn't enough. She went to the large fireplace, happy to find that some of the embers were still glowing. It wouldn't take much for the fire to get going again but when she went to retrieve wood from the storage beside the fireplace, she noticed just how low she was running. Obviously Lukas had used some the night before and again to get the stove going, but that left her with very little and when she walked to the back door of the cabin and peered outside, everything was covered in a thick layer of snow. Where on earth would she find more wood? They were supposed to have left this morning. This was never meant to have been a concern for her.

'I could go outside and look for more logs,' she mumbled to herself, but her ankle was still tender, so she could run into trouble. The last thing she needed or wanted was Lukas's help again. She'd only just got rid of him.

He left in this weather to walk to his cabin.

'That's not my problem!' she half yelled. 'He could have been pleasant but he never is.' She walked away from the door. 'It's fine. I need to keep what I have for that stove.' She glanced over at the large cast iron appliance. The red-gold flame dancing behind the glass. She had never used one of these things before. When Lukas had asked her to get the fire going she had been lost. She'd tried looking it up on her phone but with no cell service it had been impossible, but she hadn't been able to admit that to him. For now, she had a source of heat but the stove was useless to her because unless she was scrambling eggs or making ramen, she was an utterly incompetent cook. It never seemed like something she needed to waste time learning. Not when she lived in London and travelled for work all the time.

'Okay, Katherine, think. The storm is dying, so it won't be long before someone comes back. The team's equipment is still here.' That got her racing towards the bedrooms. 'So are their clothes.' She rummaged through the cupboard, finding a big thick jacket. 'Perfect!'

She threw off her jacket and pulled on one of the sweaters and then the jacket, almost immediately finding relief from the chill.

'Snacks.' That was next on the list. She hadn't brought any. There had been no need. They'd only been meant to be there for two nights. Katherine especially wouldn't have needed snacks when she was so disciplined about how she ate. But discipline didn't matter now. She rummaged through the kitchen cupboards finding a box of granola bars. Tearing one open, she devoured it right there before taking another and huddling on the couch. Knees to her chest. Her arms wrapped around herself.

Hopefully they would all come back soon.

Lukas fought his way into his cabin, brushing the snow off his clothes the moment he closed the door. With no fires going, the cabin was cold. A sacrifice made to ensure Katherine's safety. And all he'd gotten for his trouble was more accusations hurled at him. But she was alive and that was all he really needed.

Even though the woman had a way of getting under his skin.

He'd never met a more stubbornly proud person.

Well, now she could take care of herself since she so clearly wanted to. She was no longer any of his concern. He had done the right thing and now he could wait in the comfort of his own space.

He started a fire in the fireplace before doing the same in the kitchen. He was ravenous. It had been nearly a full day since he had eaten anything and even longer since he'd worked out. Working out would have to wait as much as it annoyed him. It set his day off-kilter. But it already was off-kilter, thanks to Katherine. He needed a shower and then food.

Mercifully, there was still warm water. When he stripped off his clothes and stepped under the jets, his body relaxed. His muscles had been tense; bunched for a whole day, it felt like he had let go of a weight now. And in the warm, relaxing water, his mind drifted. Images of toned, milky skin and red hair flashed behind his eyes making him groan. Streams of water ran down his arms over hands that clenched as he remembered Katherine's softness. It was cruel that his body would react so readily to her when he hated her so much. But there was no arguing with how attractive he found her when the evidence of that was hard and throbbing.

He shut off the taps with an irritated growl. After changing into clean, warm clothes, he made his way back into the kitchen and pulled ingredients from the cupboards and fridge to make the same breakfast he started every day with. He enjoyed cooking. It reminded him of his father and it was easier to remain in the peak physical condition needed for racing if he prepared his food himself.

Lukas meticulously added the ingredients to a saucepan, stirring it on the heat until it was thick and rich, then poured the hot porridge with berries and honey into a bowl adding a few more berries on top. He placed a spoon into the bowl but he couldn't lift it to his lips. Katherine hadn't even tried to make a drink before he left. Did she have anything at all to eat? Why did he care? Why should her well-being affect whether or not he could dive into his steaming hot breakfast?

He let out a long string of expletives. Why couldn't he get her out of his head? And why on earth did the air crackle whenever they were together? He felt it every time. Had felt it the moment he looked at her in the press pen three years ago. Time had turned to sludge that day. In his mind, he could still see her as she'd looked then in the VelociTV kit. A headset clamped over her ears, but her red hair still fluttering in the breeze. Clear blue eyes sparkling as the light caught them. A microphone in her slender hand, gold ring shining on her finger. And a smile on her lips that had stopped him in his tracks.

He'd known instantly he couldn't talk to her, he couldn't have allowed himself an attraction to a member of the media. Not when his relationship to the woman he loved and should have married had come to such a hurtful end right before.

You need to figure this thing out with the media because they are never going away, but I am.

The last thing he'd wanted was another relationship to hide and protect from them. So he hadn't allowed himself to get into Katherine's orbit. What would that spark have turned into? A charge so intense, like they'd harnessed the very lightning. Whether he was attracted to her or hated her.

Lukas had read about crackling hate between people and always dismissed it as fantastical but maybe there was truth in it. Maybe what he had initially felt was her undiluted hatred towards him. Why else would she attack him so consistently? He hadn't even said a word to her.

Right there was a perfect reason why he shouldn't care about Katherine.

Cursing loudly, he pushed his bowl away and grabbed his jacket, doing it up firmly before stepping back out into the storm.

'This is ridiculous,' he muttered, risking his life as he stomped through the wind and snow towards her cabin. A cabin she should have been sharing. It was ridiculous that he was taking any risk for this woman who would see his dream, all that he and his father had worked for, crash and burn. She would never understand what that was like.

When he reached her door, he was well and truly in a black mood.

He tried the handle and found that it was unlocked. 'Seriously? She's alone and she couldn't even lock this.'

Again, why do you care?

He ignored the voice.

He entered into the large living space and Katherine's head snapped in his direction, Her expression going from shock to suspicion. But he didn't react. He was too busy looking at what she wore. Bundled on the couch in a too-big jacket with Aero TV embroidered on the sleeve and a sweater that was just as big under it, she was holding her-self around her knees. He had seen that jacket before. She was wearing one of the cameraman's clothes and he hated it, but he couldn't understand why. At least she was warm now. So why was it so irritating?

The cabin was warmer now but nowhere near as com-fortable as his. And when he looked around he didn't see a cup or mug or plate. The stovetop too was bare but he did spot an empty wrapper on the table beside the couch.

'Is that all you've had to eat?' he asked her, trying very hard to keep his voice even.

'What's it to you?' she challenged.

'Answer the question, Katherine,' he said through grit-ted teeth.

'Yes, but I don't see how that's any of your business.'

Honestly, could she be more aggravating? He should leave. He had checked on her, she was alive, so now he could go and enjoy his hot food.

But if she had no food here, he couldn't just leave her.

'I've already said I don't want your death on my con-science,' Lukas replied. 'Get your things, I'm taking you to my cabin.'

'Why?' Katherine asked, making no attempt to move.

'Because it's warm and I have food.'

'Don't bother yourself. The storm is dying down, so the others will return soon.' She turned away from him to look at the fireplace, which had nothing but ash in it.

'We won't be seeing anyone for a few days. They don't know that we're here. They think we're out there somewhere,' he said, pointing at the door, 'because you ran off, which was an irresponsible thing to do. They won't risk any lives in this weather. Helicopters can't fly in this. There's no visibility and they will likely organise a search before they come back here and only when it is safe to do so. So, you will stay with me because you are useless at survival. Get your things and let's go.'

Katherine stared at him. The air grew thicker and thicker until it felt like he couldn't breathe it in, but he wasn't backing down. If she didn't listen, he would carry her out.

Do it, his body begged but he stood resolutely where he was.

'Fine.'

She disappeared from the room and he collected whatever food he could carry to his cabin to keep them alive. He waited an eternity that was truthfully only a few minutes, and Katherine returned rolling a small hardshell bag behind her.

'Let's go,' Lukas said, taking the bag from her and leading her through the snow into his cabin. 'Leave your coat and shoes by the door,' he instructed as they entered, 'and then sit in front of the fire.' It was so much warmer in here. With their coats hanging up, they would be warm and dry the next time they had to put them on.

'What smells so good?' Katherine asked, listening to him without complaint for once.

'Porridge and berries. Would you like some?'

'I would, but didn't you make it for yourself?' He watched her wring her hands, clearly uncomfortable to be in his space. A small, uncharitable part of him was glad of it.

'I did but I can make more.'

'Thank you,' she said, looking around as she made her way to the kitchen counter with three tall bar-stools on one side. His cabin was a lot larger than the one she and the crew shared. The touches more luxurious. There were perks to being who he was.

Lukas tried to ignore Katherine. Tried to ignore when she took hold of the spoon that had so nearly touched his lips, and ate his food. Tried to ignore her quiet moan and the way her eyes fluttered shut.

Tried and failed.

That sound, that expression was saved to his memory.

He forced himself to turn away and make another portion but all the while he could feel her eyes on him.

'You make that look so effortless,' she murmured, but he didn't turn to look. Instead, he kept his eyes firmly on the contents of the saucepan.

'What? Cooking?'

He heard no response, so he was forced to look at her, finding her eyes locked on to his hands. This was probably the longest they had ever interacted without sniping at each other. *I wonder how long it will last.*

'Can't you cook?'

Again, he got no response.

'I'll take that as a no, then.'

He stood where he was, the counter between them, and practically inhaled the bowl of food. Katherine had done the same.

'Thank you, that was really good.'

Lukas could see how hard it was for her to pay him the compliment.

'How do you know how to cook? I wouldn't have pegged you for the type.'

Lukas's heart constricted painfully. 'My father was a cook. He taught me.'

He saw her eyes light up with curiosity. It made her look breathtaking and darkened his mood further because this was exactly what he hated. People learning something small about him and then hungering for more information that they had no business to know.

'I thought your father was a mechanic.'

Lukas looked into his empty bowl. So much of the person he was was thanks to his father. His discipline, his skill. His preparedness. The reason he had extra provisions now was thanks to lessons his father had taught him. Know the risks and plan around them. 'He was both. He worked two jobs to support my racing career. Three, if you count how hard he worked to get me sponsors.' He chuffed. Anger curled in his stomach because the world already knew about his family. Neither he nor his father had had any privacy. 'Why ask about him when you already know? When you and everyone like you already went digging around in my past for a bit of juicy gossip?'

He picked up his bowl and tossed it into the sink with a loud clang. His pulse rushed in his ears as he remembered stories about his parents' divorce and his strained relationship with his mother being splashed around, forcing him to relive the agony of his family breaking apart. The fact that he was the reason they'd divorced in the first place. It was his fault, and he'd had to see it day after day for months.

He felt a hand grip his arm, making him turn around. Katherine's cheeks were red. Her lips thin.

'Don't you dare act like a victim when you're ruthless too.' Her voice was pitched low.

He stepped closer to her. That crackle was back. As though whatever this was between them would generate bolts that would tear the very cabin apart. 'What have I ever done that could even remotely be as unscrupulous as your actions?' He fought so hard not to raise his voice. Not to let her get under his skin but she'd burrowed there already. Katherine was the itch he could never get rid off.

'Are you joking right now?' she asked incredulously.

He had no idea what she was on about.

'You got me fired!' she yelled.

'You don't know what you're talking about.' There were a lot of media personalities Lukas didn't like but he had never used his power to get anyone fired. Especially not Katherine. He had, however, secretly tried to help her. Not that he would ever tell her that. Katherine probably wouldn't believe him if he did. And he certainly didn't want her to think that he *needed* her to think better of him.

'I don't know what I'm talking about?' She pushed him, hands on his chest. Her eyes glossy and bloodshot. 'You told my producer you didn't want to talk to me. Just me! It was a boys' club! They were just looking for a reason to get rid of me, and you handed them one. And why? Because I'm a woman? You're like all the other misogynists—just like your friend Roman—who want to keep the sport male-dominated, which is *so* incredibly hypocritical when your publicist is a woman. Or are you only happy to address the imbalance when it suits you?'

Lukas was shocked. First, Roman wasn't his friend. Lukas tolerated him at best. And second, he remembered those words, but he'd said them to Dominic, right after the very sight of Katherine had rendered him speechless.

Only after he'd said the words had he realised Katherine's producer had heard him. He had even spoken to him, explained that it wasn't Katherine's fault. The producer had said it was fine.

Clearly it hadn't been fine.

But that didn't mean Lukas wasn't angry. Angry that Katherine hadn't come to him so they could clear the air. She hadn't known him and had assumed the worst from the very start. A person could only think so ill of another if they were already willing to believe that of them.

'Believe whatever you want,' he snapped, turning to leave.

'What I believe is true.'

Lukas laughed at that. A short burst of air clearly telling Katherine what he thought of that.

'I bet you're one of those people who underpays her compared to the male publicists too. Tell me, what were you paid in this last season after your bonuses?'

Lukas was tired of playing this game. This was public knowledge much to his dismay. 'Sixty-nine million euros.' The extent of his endorsement deals wasn't known so Katherine wouldn't learn about it now either.

'Sixty-nine, how appropriate for the man who will do anything.'

Lukas had had enough. She thought she knew so much about him, every single thing she knew was wrong. 'How much sex do you think I have?' he asked, doing nothing to temper his annoyance.

'Please,' Katherine scoffed, 'don't insult my intelligence. I've seen the number of women you appear with.'

Only because the media wouldn't give him an ounce of privacy and every time he had a dinner or arrived at an event a picture was taken. None of those women were ever in a relationship with him. 'Appear with. Not sleep with. Not date. My tastes in all things are very exacting.'

Katherine let out a taunting laugh. 'Okay, I'll bite. How many months has it been exactly?'

Knowing it would shut her up, Lukas leaned down. His lips brushed the shell of her ear. He felt the shiver that passed through her, the touch sparking as if they were statically charged. 'Three years.' He pulled away, smug at the shock on her face. 'What's wrong?' he asked venomously, 'Upset that it doesn't fit the narrative of me you're trying to peddle?'

Katherine was rendered mute. There were no comebacks. Satisfied, angry and tense, Lukas left her standing in the kitchen and walked away.

CHAPTER SIX

KATHERINE WATCHED LUKAS'S retreating back, breathing heavily. She'd never stooped so low as to attack a person the way she had Lukas right then but he made her crazy. As if she couldn't keep whatever she was feeling—anger, frustration, irritation—inside her when he was around. It all burst out of her in the most uncontrolled way and she hated that she could hardly temper what she said before she said it.

She had seen plenty of pictures of Lukas with women. They were almost never posed for. People talked. She wasn't the only one who had those ideas about him. That was no excuse though. As shocked as she was at his revelation, there was no denying he was telling the truth. No faking the offense he had taken, that flash of hurt in his eyes. Clearly something had happened there and she regretted her actions.

But she couldn't talk to him.

Not yet.

He had taken no responsibility for getting her fired. She couldn't forgive that. So here she was, upset at herself but still so angry at Lukas that she didn't know what to do with all this hate.

Her legs were finally able to move. They carried her to

the door, but where would she go? A walk would help her cool off but a walk in a blizzard would get her killed. She could go back to her cabin and get some space but what then? She didn't really have much in the way of food or heat. And it was warm here. She felt infinitely better for having had something real to eat. Lukas didn't have to bring her here but he had. Even when he detested her as much as she did him.

Heaving a great big sigh, Katherine sat in front of the fireplace, staring at the hypnotic way the flames swayed and crackled.

As much as she hated to admit it, Lukas was right. While the storm wasn't blowing as intensely, it wasn't dying down sufficiently for help to arrive and she had no idea when it would stop. They were alone out here. They needed to rely on each other, so maybe the wisest thing to do would be to put their differences aside. She could be the bigger person. She had been when she didn't expose the reason she was fired from VelociTV.

Calmer, Katherine pushed off the floor and went looking for Lukas, which was harder than she had anticipated. She opened several doors in the cabin, finding a sauna, a gym, an entertainment room, a room with a large pool table in the middle. Finally, she tried a locked door and knocked gently on the wood.

'Lukas, can we talk?' she asked softly. 'Please.'

She heard shuffling and then the door swung inwards. Lukas stood there, one hand on the door-handle and the other on the frame. His knitted turtleneck sweater stretched across his chest, defining the incredible tone of his physique. The soft, camel colour warmed his grey eyes that so often reminded her of a winter storm, so at odds with his light brown hair.

How was this man single for three years? He was objectively rather beautiful.

She looked up into those intelligent eyes that were assessing her. He said nothing but if the roles were reversed she would probably do the same.

'I just want to talk,' Katherine said, waiting for a response. Most likely a rejection. He pushed through the doorway and just before he could close the door, she spied a book lying face down on the king-size bed.

She really didn't think he was the reading type, but she hadn't thought he could cook, nor had she realised that he would be good at survival. He had gone looking for her equipped with a rope, had prevented hypothermia from setting in. There was a man behind the racer that she truly did not know.

He led her to the closest room. She took a seat on one of the buttery-soft tan leather couches and patted the cushion, hoping he would join her. See that she could be civil. To her relief he accepted, pouring himself onto the couch and draping his arm over the back-rest but he didn't look at her. He kept his eyes fixed to the black screen of the large television mounted on the wall.

Well, it looked like she would be doing all the talking.

'I'm sorry for what I said earlier, Lukas, it wasn't my finest moment.' All he did was blink but she could tell he was listening, so she ploughed on. 'I want to propose a truce.'

He looked at her then. Icy eyes piercing into hers. A shiver ran down her spine and she found herself leaning towards them just a little. She tried to pull away but couldn't.

'What do you think it was when I got you from that cabin, fed and warmed you?' She had never heard his voice so low. So robotic.

'I…' What could she say? That she didn't want to believe he could do anything kind or decent. 'I didn't see it for what it was,' she admitted. 'The attitude didn't help,' she added.

'Fine. So you want a truce. What does that mean?'

'It means that you're right, we're stuck here together and maybe we should work together to survive. I'll admit that I am lacking in some skills, but I can make up for them in other ways. All you need to do is teach me and I can help. It will be a lot easier if we coexist peacefully than if we're at each other's throats all the time.'

'Can *you* do that?' He turned towards her, folding one leg under the other as he focussed all his attention on her.

Can I…ugh, why is he so insufferable? It took a Herculean effort not to snap at him. 'I can try if you try too.'

He looked like he was thinking about it. It wasn't lost on Katherine that he could kick her out and live comfortably until help arrived, but anything could happen out here, and it wouldn't be smart to be apart when they could only rely on each other's help.

'I can agree to that. It's just until we're rescued, then we go back to our lives,' he said.

'Absolutely.' Katherine held out her hand. Lukas looked at it before he took it in his own much larger, warmer one, and shook it, scorching her skin. She did well to hide her gasp and pulled her hand away.

As she flexed her fingers, she caught a flash of something in Lukas's eyes that she didn't want to question.

Katherine was surprised but pleased by how well she and Lukas did over the days that followed. He did well to measure his tone when he spoke to her and cooked all their meals.

In turn, she tried not to remember that he'd gotten her fired, which helped a great deal in them being civil. It didn't help her blood pressure though. Being around Lukas was a constant reminder of what he had done. A constant reminder of the misogyny she faced. Of what her relationship with her father might become if she ever lost this career.

It made her burn, but they had a truce. A truce that ensured her survival, so as angry as she often found herself, as frustrated and bitter…she had to take a deep breath and force it all down. Still, her heart felt like it was constantly beating in her ears. Her stomach was constantly in knots. Even sleep was proving difficult.

The truce was temporary and soon they would escape each other.

Katherine was adding wood to the stove, feeding the fire, which was easy once Lukas had shown her how. And while she did that, he prepared their lunch.

'Thank you,' he said when she closed the door to the firebox.

'Can I help with lunch?' she asked, leaning over the counter.

'You want to help?' Lukas raised an eyebrow, incredulous. 'We have to be able to eat it afterwards.'

She wished he never knew of her weakness. She was preparing to throw a barb of her own when she noticed the corner of his lips kicked up in the most delicious way and realised he was teasing her.

'Don't be an ass or I'll eat all the yoghurt,' she retorted, forcing herself to calm down.

'Too late for that and you can help with the vegetables. Do you know what to do?'

'I've watched you enough.' She was watching him right

now. The way he rubbed the marinade he had made with their limited ingredients over the chicken breasts. It was not normal to stare at his hands like this, so she yanked open the fridge. He was right, the yogurt had gone. In fact, a lot of the food had diminished. They were starting to run alarmingly low. Every meal was much smaller than Katherine knew he would really need. Obviously, he had to be mindful about how he rationed the groceries to feed them both. His supplies had been meant to be for him alone for no more than a couple days and the food he'd taken from the crew's cabin had been meant to feed them for two more meals.

'You know,' he said as she began chopping, 'that day in the paddock, I was talking to Dominic. I hadn't realised that your producer overheard what I said at first.'

Katherine stopped breathing. Her knife pausing on the board. Her heart beat rapidly. They had avoided this subject since their argument.

'When I did, I told him discreetly that what he heard wasn't your fault. It had nothing to do with you. I told him that I couldn't explain further than that and he said he understood. I knew they fired you. I didn't know why.'

She handed her chopping board to him, careful to avoid his touch, careful to hide her shaking.

When he bent to place the dish in the oven, she asked, 'Why didn't you want to talk to me? We hadn't met before that point.'

Lukas closed the oven door, regret etched onto his face. 'It doesn't matter why. I'm sorry that it happened.'

There they were. The words she had wanted to hear for so long. She'd wanted to make him take responsibility for what he'd done to her and when he did she was never going to accept the apology. Was never going to forgive him. She hadn't once considered that he could somehow be innocent, or that his words were taken out of context. She had seen him speak into the ear of her producer.

'I didn't realise—that's not what he—' Katherine's mind was racing. 'Did you ever find out what he said to me? Did he tell you?'

'No,' Lukas said, stepping closer, 'because I don't grant interviews to VelociTV. I give them none of my time.'

'Why?' She had to know. Was it because of her? But that would be ridiculous wouldn't it because Lukas hated her and it had been three years. 'Why, Lukas?'

'It's not important. The point is that I didn't know.'

It mattered to her. It shouldn't but it did. Though, given the fact that Lukas was turning away from her, she knew she wouldn't get an answer even if she needed it.

'Take a seat. I'll bring the food out when it's done.'

She was being dismissed. Why was he so opposed to talking about this? What was he hiding? Was she reading too much into it? She wanted to grab him by the arm and make him look into her eyes and spill his secrets. But she remembered the last time they'd touched, the handshake that still made her skin tingle when she thought about it, and she couldn't risk the move.

They ate in silence. Side by side. The atmosphere neither comfortable nor hostile for once. It felt like they were on the verge of something. Like words sitting on the tip of a tongue but refusing to fall. And when they were done and the place had been perfectly tidied—as she had learned Lukas needed—she sat in front of the fireplace fully expecting Lukas to disappear into one of the other rooms as he so often did. Except he didn't.

He joined her on the couch, wrapping a blanket around both their shoulders, huddling close as if he knew that having a smaller fire and the anxiety from the situation had chilled her. But having his body so close raised everything. Her awareness. Her heart rate. Her temperature. They weren't hating on each other now, so why was he still affecting her like this?

'Thank you for apologising earlier,' she said softly. She still wanted him to know what he had jeopardised without even knowing it. Or maybe it was that she was feeling rather alone with nothing but white beyond the windows and only Lukas for company. Maybe it was that she had gone longer than usual without talking to her father. Whatever the reason, she wanted to talk now. 'I was hurt but I was also terrified when I lost that job.'

'Why?'

'Because it was a dream I shared with my father and I was afraid I'd lost it before I even really had a chance to enjoy it.' A tremor passed through her at the memory and, mistaking that for cold, Lukas wrapped an arm around her, holding her to his body. But she didn't correct him. Didn't pull away. She wanted to stay exactly where she was.

What is happening?

'I come from a fairly large family. I have an older brother, a younger brother and a twin sister, and try as I might, I could never relate to them. They all got along so well but I was so different. Quiet. Studious. I preferred my books to company, while they were all so extroverted. The lives of the party. They had their little club and I was not part of it, which was fine because I had my own interests. I used to hang out in the library, they used to get into trouble. My sister, Paige, especially. And that has never changed. But through all of that, my dad and I had something to bond over. Something that only interested the two of us and that was Alpha One racing. During qualifying and the race, my dad was only mine for the entire broadcast. When it was over he had to go back to putting out the fires the others caused.' Katherine had seen how her siblings' behaviour would stress out her parents and she was determined that they would never have to worry about her. She still lived by that code as her parents were getting older. They had retirements to think about but how could they with three of their children still staying with them?

'Racing wasn't a realistic dream for you to have,' Lukas said. There was no judgement or mockery. It was a simple, unfortunate truth.

'No. Not just because there weren't any real avenues for female racers at the time but also, there would have been no way for them to support me financially. But journalism? That was something I could work towards and my father was always my biggest supporter. He celebrated every step with me.' And Katherine lived for that attention. It was the only time she felt seen.

'What about your mother?'

That was a lot more complicated to answer. While Katherine loved her mother, she was probably the reason Katherine was so set on never marrying. Never having children. Her mother's pressure still fuelled her drive in the opposite direction.

'My mother doesn't understand my need to succeed at all costs.' Katherine supposed the one person who could understand that was sitting next to her. 'She had a very promising career in marketing. She was climbing the corporate ladder and making a name for herself in the company but then she got married and had children. She left her corporate job for a lower paying one with limited growth that gave her time to spend with the family.'

Lukas's arm tightened fractionally. 'What's the "but"?'

'*But* she didn't spend much of it with me because I didn't need it as much as the others. She wants me to settle down like she did because, to her, that's the right way to do things. Pursue things when you're young and unattached but then make sacrifices for a family.' But to Katherine the sacrifices always seemed too big.

She had seen pictures of her mother from her corporate days. A sophisticated, polished woman. Stylish and elegant. She had seen her parents' wedding pictures where her mother had four bridesmaids. Her closest friends. Katherine hadn't met a single one of them in person and knew her mother had lost touch with them. The lack of time due to their chaotic family was to blame. Katherine knew it.

That bright sophisticated woman was gone, replaced by one run off her feet. Styled hair replaced by an untidy bun every day. The only people her mother spoke to daily were her husband and her children. Excluding Katherine, of course, because Katherine didn't need tending to. Her mother claimed happiness and yet, when they were younger, Katherine had seen the longing way she used to look at the handful of corporate mums who would drop their kids off in a hurry for school. On the weekends, when Paige used to flip through magazines, Katherine had noticed the way her mother—her own clothes covered in splatters from cooking or taking care of Nicholas—would gaze longingly at the fashion. The glamazons so reflective of how she once looked.

Her mother wasn't fulfilled but she had an unshakeable idea of what duty meant. Of what her role was. And for some reason she wanted Katherine to follow suit.

'And what do you want?' Lukas asked.

'I want to establish myself so firmly that no one thinks about Alpha One broadcasting without thinking about me.

I want to follow this circus for the rest of my life. I want to grow bigger than I am. I want to—'

'You want to…' Lukas urged.

'I want to be successful. I want to take care of my parents when they're older. I know I'll have to, with Paige the way she is.'

Katherine looked up at Lukas and saw understanding on his face.

'They must be proud of you,' he said. 'Whether they show it or not.'

'I don't know,' Katherine admitted. 'Before coming here I was meant to have dinner with my family but they cancelled because Paige got into trouble.'

'Is it always like that?'

'Yes, but I understand. The others need my parents' support more than I do.'

Lukas shook his head. 'It shouldn't have to be that way, but I understand.'

'You do?'

The world knew about his parents' divorce, about his strained relationship with his mother, because tabloids had reported on it, but he was so private, more than that was purely a guess.

'My mother left because of me.'

Katherine's heart stuttered to a stop.

'My father spent a lot of time, energy and money on my racing. All those things could have been spent on the family and we could have had a more comfortable life.'

Katherine knew Lukas had come from humble beginnings. Everyone did. Just as everyone knew his father. A man who was at as many races as he could attend, which was nearly all of them until his death.

'Having to support a child through karting and everything else puts a huge financial burden on a family. My mother didn't sign up for that, so she divorced him and moved to Salzburg.'

Katherine put her arms around Lukas's middle, holding him tightly. If someone had told her days ago that she would be trying to offer him comfort she would have laughed in their face. But here they were and she realised something: They weren't so different.

'It was difficult but we were fine. My dad and I had each other until just over a year ago.' Lukas stopped talking. The anguish in his expression was hard to witness and even harder to feel. And she could feel it. As if her own heart was trying to tear itself to pieces.

Katherine remembered when Florian Jäger had died. It had been a short illness. Lukas had done absolutely no PR in the weeks leading up to his death. The whole paddock knew he was flying back and forth each night just to see his father while he could. Her stomach churned with guilt now because she remembered calling into question if Lukas would be able to remain competitive in the build-up to the race the next day. If it was her father who died and that was what people had said afterwards, she would have likely set the world on fire. But she'd had to ask the question. It was on everyone's lips. Up and down the paddock. Online. At the network.

Katherine realised that at every turn she had assumed the worst about Lukas. She hadn't been good to him. But she couldn't apologise, because she'd only been doing her job.

'I'm not sure why I told you that.' It seemed like he said that more to himself than her.

'Because we're running low on wood and food and might succumb to the elements and die while in this over-the-top cabin,' she joked, hoping to bring some levity to the atmosphere that had grown solemn. And when she heard him chuckle, she felt an odd sort of relief.

'Are you comfortable?' he asked.

She adjusted against him. 'Mmm-hmm.' Then she glanced up and found him looking down at her. And she was caught. Frozen in place by a wintery gaze. One that reeled her in as if she were hypnotised. Her lips parted and so did his. Pink and soft. His breath hit her face. Cool and minty. He was so close now. Any movement might make their lips brush.

Just as they were about to touch, he pulled away. Blinking fast as if to clear away an enchantment. He pulled the blanket tighter around them, which forced her upright, breaking the connection of their bodies, and looked away.

What was that?

CHAPTER SEVEN

LUKAS'S HEART HAD thrummed in his chest. His skin had felt red-hot everywhere that Katherine had touched him. It was as if she'd ignited him and he'd burned up like flash paper.

And he was coming to see that she had brought out this reaction in him in every heated exchange. In every thought. Every touch. He'd needed to break the connection of their bodies and had done so, but he couldn't move away, because it was a thrill to be so close to her. Because she was cold and anxious. Because of all that she had told him.

So he stayed on the couch, under the blanket, with her. Sat with her in silence until they dozed off.

And when he finally opened his eyes to find the fire grown low, adding a log or two was not his first thought. Not when he looked beside him and found Katherine curled towards him in her sleep. With her head on his shoulder and her hands pressed under her cheek. Peaceful. Beautiful. Dangerous.

She was off-limits to him. He shouldn't want to brush her cheek or kiss her lips but he had wanted to earlier. He still wanted to.

He needed space. Air.

Laying Katherine down on the cushions as gently as possible, he extricated himself from the blanket and tucked her in tightly. Then he threw a couple logs on the fire and looked out the window. The wind had died down. The snow was no longer falling. The night sky lay beyond the filmiest of wispy clouds that were slowly blowing away.

He needed air and now he could get it.

He shoved his feet into his snow-boots and tugged on his jacket as he stepped out onto the porch. Nothing but thick, untouched snow lit up in a hint of silver from the crescent moon as far as the eye could see. The trees were like glittering pillars of white. Only the very edges of their needles poked through the pillowy snow that stood out in stark contrast to the black, shimmering night sky.

Lukas took a deep breath.

And then another.

And another.

Being away from Katherine cleared his head a little. He hadn't realised that it had happened but in the days they'd been together she had taken over his every thought. A pervasive presence. A woman he didn't want to be around and yet he so clearly did.

'How can you want to kiss her after all she's done?' he asked in the still night.

He would have loved to know the answer. Why did his body feel like it was breaking to get the smallest of touches? He hated her. *Hated* her.

It wasn't always that way.

No, it wasn't. The image of the first time he saw her lived in his head. The way she'd taken his breath away. There has always been something between them. Something electric. Something chemical. Something highly reactive to even the smallest stimulus. He couldn't deny that.

Lukas looked back at the closed door of the cabin. Part of him wanted to go back in there. Sit beside her pretending it was nothing, but inside he knew what it would be: an adrenaline junkie seeking out the thrill.

He turned away to lean against one of the large posts and as he looked up, he saw the night sky shift. Light slowly dancing across the heavens. Muted and nearly white but the longer he stared at it the brighter it became. Brush strokes of pink and green dancing overhead between Lukas and the stars. It was breathtaking.

And he wanted Katherine to witness it with him.

He ran inside and knelt beside the couch.

'Katherine.' He fought and lost the urge to run the backs of his fingers down her cheek.

She mumbled sleepily making him smile. She was rather adorable like this.

'I think you'll want to see this.'

'What is it?' she slurred.

'The aurora.'

Her eyes flew open. 'What?'

He laughed at her reaction and fetched her snow-boots, slipping them onto her feet and then bundling her tighter in the blankets. 'Come on.'

He led her outside and held her back to his body, making sure her blanket didn't slip, keeping her warm. 'Look up.'

The lights were flaring beautifully now. Streaks of colour feathering to the heavens while jagged lines swirled and snaked against the black canvas of the sky.

'Wow,' Katherine breathed. 'Thank you for getting me. It's stunning.'

And then he looked at her. Saw the wonder in her blue eyes. The soft smile on her lips. She turned and caught him staring. Her smile growing full and contagious, stealing his breath.

'You're not looking at the sky.'

'I can't.' Pure honesty fell from his lips before he could think about what he was saying. But he couldn't take it back. Katherine was smart. She knew exactly what he meant. And he was sure his heart ceased functioning altogether when she turned in his arms. The smile dropping off her face as she searched his. Her eyes touching every inch of his skin before trapping his gaze. Something was sparking between them, and they were tinder catching alight. They couldn't fight it any longer. Not when they were moving closer, when their breaths mingled, when their lips touched and every explosive interaction, all that fire and electricity had somewhere to go.

Katherine gasped and Lukas wasn't sure if the sound he made was a moan, an anguished wail, a curse or prayer. Maybe it was all those things. His arms banded around her just as her hands peeked out of her blanket to fist the front of his jacket. And he kissed her. Slowly but desperately. Hungrily but savouring. Her taste consuming. Her tongue against his setting off a series of explosions in his body. Making him hard. Needy. Ravenous. And when she angled her head, he brought his hand up to the nape of her neck, holding her in place while he kissed her deeply. Losing control. Licking the roof of her mouth. His tongue dancing with hers. His teeth catching her bottom lip, and he ripped himself away.

He took two steps back and turned away from her. Adrenaline flooded his body. This was how he felt when he threw himself out of a plane, or went skiing off piste, or when he caught his car from spinning at three hundred kilometres an hour.

He was alive.

Katherine made him feel like this.

He shouldn't be surprised. Hate was a passionate emotion and there was unbridled passion here.

Do you really hate her?

No. He didn't. Not anymore.

He gripped his hair at the roots, then spun around and saw her watching him.

Every shackle broke loose.

Katherine saw the moment Lukas threw caution to the wind. He closed the distance between them. Everything about him screaming hunter. A silver-eyed wolf. But she wasn't prey. The moment he was within reach, she grabbed the front of his jacket and tugged him to her. She kissed him the same instant his hands cradled her face, breathing him in just as she heard him inhale this kiss. His lips were urgent but so were her hands and then he was spinning them around. Pushing her against the thick post. His body pressed against hers. Her stomach was in her throat. Chest heaving. Moisture pooling her core. Teeth and tongues clashing. Uncontrolled, just like they always were.

Whether they were arguing or kissing, there was never any controlling what they brought out in each other. And she wanted to touch him. Wanted him to call out her name and to make him beg, but there was no getting through his bloody jacket, and yet she felt his hands push through the gap in the blanket and slide under her top. His hands, surprisingly warm, left a path of tingles in their wake that had nothing to do with the temperature of their skin.

And then they were moving again but she stepped on the blanket and Lukas growled in frustration. Picking her up bridal-style, he took her back inside.

'The sky is beautiful right now, but I have no patience in me,' he said, teeth grazing her neck.

'I don't want you to be patient,' she confessed breathlessly. She just wanted him. He always heightened what she felt. It was no different when the sensations were physical. The moment he set her on her feet, she threw off the blanket, and his hands were pulling up on her top and pushing down on her leggings, desperate to get to her skin. But she understood because she was shoving him out of that jacket and tearing at his sweater. Lukas bent down, allowing her to yank it off his head.

Katherine had seen many impressive athletes in her life, but she was ill prepared for the perfection of Lukas's lean, cut body. Every muscle defined, hard and exquisite. And yet his skin was so soft, as if silk had been poured over a perfect frame to form him.

'Enjoying the view?'

She grinned. 'Yes.' She had always been brutally honest with him, there was no reason to hide her thoughts now.

That moment was all Lukas gave her before finally pulling her top off and laying her in front of the fire on the thick, fluffy rug. His fingers slid beneath the waistband of her leggings and underwear alike, pulling them both off in one. And then he was kissing her…there.

Everything was moving so fast but not fast enough. She wanted his lips on hers and his hardness inside her. There was heat in her veins and lightning in her belly. Lukas's tongue sent sparks of pure pleasure throughout her body but she wanted more. More. More.

Gripping his hair, she lifted his head off her. His eyes were half-lidded, drunk on the pleasure that was intoxicating her, and placing her hand under his chin, she urged him up her body but she didn't have to ask for what she wanted; he knew. He kissed her with a ferocity, holding himself up on his arms, allowing her hands to go to his pants and undo the belt, button and zip without looking. He shoved all the layers off him.

Finally, he was naked.

Gloriously so.

Impressively so.

God, this man should be on display in a museum.

'Glad you think so,' he said into her ear and she flushed red, realising she had spoken the words aloud. He sucked on a spot on her neck and she moaned out loud.

'Make that sound again,' he instructed. He begged.

His tongue teased the same spot, but this time his hands travelled down her body, his fingers parting her sex, slipping in.

'Lukas,' she moaned louder.

'Mmm, that's even better,' he said, voice like gravel. He pulled his fingers away and brought them up between them, showing Katherine that they were drenched. And then he licked them clean. She couldn't take it anymore.

'Dammit, Lukas, give me what I want,' she demanded.

'And what's that?' he taunted.

'You inside me.' She couldn't breathe. She needed relief from the assault of pleasure on her senses.

'I don't have a condom, Katherine,' he admitted in a seductive voice.

'You can't leave me like this,' she begged. She was certain she would cry if he stopped now.

'I have no intention to. I'm happy to feast.' He licked his pink lips and she blushed to her roots.

'I'm on the pill and you haven't been with anyone in three years.' A fact she trusted because Lukas always spoke the truth. He was blunt and seemed like he didn't care how his words landed so there was no reason to doubt him now. Regardless of how much she hated him, his integrity was undeniable.

The thought made her realise something: She didn't hate him anymore.

'The pill wouldn't make a difference anyway,' he said against her skin. His fingers teasing her once again. 'Are you sure?'

'Yes,' she panted. 'I want you now.'

Lukas didn't need telling twice and thrust his hard, throbbing cock into her. She gasped loudly, arching her back. And then he raised her leg and set a pace that made her light-headed. High. Her lungs were no longer adequately functioning and each of his growls and curses and pants raised goose bumps on her skin. Made her heart skip beats.

This was beyond anything she could have imagined. He kept pushing her higher, higher, higher. Like a firework rising above the clouds.

'Come for me, Katherine,' he commanded, and she exploded around him in pyrotechnic glory. Lukas, her pyromaniac, was close behind. He slid his large hand under her head, holding her forehead to his, cursing out her name as his body tensed, his muscles lower down undulating in waves until he could finally take a breath. Until he relaxed and let her leg down. Until he finally opened his eyes. They were molten silver.

'Lukas,' she breathed, scarcely able to believe what they'd done or how incredible it felt or how badly she wanted to do it again.

'I know,' he replied.

CHAPTER EIGHT

KATHERINE FOUND HERSELF in the entertainment room, an inviting warmly coloured space. She ran her fingertips along the edge of the polished pool table. Picked up a ball, testing the weight of it.

She had left a sleeping Lukas in front of the fire. In the aftermath of them having sex, she hadn't been able to rest. She couldn't stop thinking about how crazed they were for each other. How perfectly they fit. How he had been the best she had ever slept with. How frantic they had been.

And then she couldn't stop thinking about what he said. *The pill wouldn't make a difference anyway.*

She didn't know what that meant but it made her think about her own choices. She didn't want love and children and sacrifice.

She fetched a wooden triangle with rounded corners hanging on the wall and brought it to the table. One by one she placed the coloured balls inside, but kept looking at the door as she did so.

'Get a grip, Katherine. The man is asleep.' But she wished he wasn't. She wished he was in this room with her and that was exactly why she needed a space to think. She stood back and looked down at the perfect J the solid balls had formed, then picked up the cue ball and took it to the top of the table.

'So this is where you are.'

She swivelled her head to find Lukas leaning against the door-frame, hands crossed over his bare chest—well, she was wearing his sweater. His jeans sat low on his hips but the button was open. His golden-brown hair was mussed from sleep and sex.

'I thought you were asleep,' she said, turning around to lean against the table.

'I was, but then I needed something and the one I needed it from was missing.'

'Oh?'

Lukas pushed off the door-frame and stalked towards her. One hand went to her face, tilting it up to him, the other grabbed her hip.

'I need this,' he said before kissing her. Instantly, she was returning it. The passion from earlier that had lowered to a simmer was at boiling point again and she couldn't get enough of him. Couldn't pull him close enough, or touch his skin enough. He was utterly intoxicating. A drug made for her. A thought that made her panic and slow the kiss to a stop. She broke away from his lips but not out of his hold.

He smiled. 'I like the way my shirt looks on you.'

She liked the way it felt on her, yet she didn't welcome the feeling. She strived to keep her romantic partners at arm's length, but she was already breaking that rule with Lukas because they were stuck together and she couldn't help learning things about him. Connecting with him. Wanting him. Wanting to know him.

Like what he said earlier.

She needed to know, especially since they had been physical.

'Can I ask you a question?'

Lukas shrugged but there was caution in his eyes.

'What did you mean earlier when you said the pill didn't matter?'

That look of caution cleared away, but Lukas still took a step back and shoved his hands into his pockets. She tracked the movement, knowing she should pay attention but his physique was distracting. She forced herself to look him in the eye as he explained.

'It wouldn't matter if you were on the pill, Katherine, because I've had a vasectomy.'

Well, that wasn't what she was expecting.

'You don't want children?' Katherine's heart was racing now. Nearly everyone in her circle criticised her choice but maybe Lukas was like her in yet another way. It made her hopeful but also wary because she really didn't need to see more ways that they were alike.

'No.' His answer was unequivocal, and it made Katherine want to cry because someone could understand her.

'I don't either,' she said through a lump in her throat.

He nodded, coming closer. 'I understand.'

'You don't need an explanation?' she whispered.

'No.' He brushed her hair behind her ear, a soft look on his face. 'You're an adult. You know best what you want and need. You don't have to explain yourself to anyone. Ever.'

Acceptance. It broke her apart and put her back together in a different way. A happier way. Now she wanted to explain to Lukas because he hadn't asked. He didn't feel entitled to tell her how to live her life, and she wanted to confide in him.

'My mother doesn't understand that. I don't want to disappoint her. She wants grandkids and is pressuring me for them, but I never want to be like her. I don't want to settle for a life that is only partially fulfilling. I don't want to give up friendships and I don't want to sacrifice my dream, my career I've worked so hard for, for a family and children that don't even appreciate or understand the sacrifice. And that's what a relationship is to me—a sacrifice. A threat to everything I've built. I don't want that. I don't even have pets. My plants are made from building blocks. I want a life where I'm free to go anywhere. Travel with Alpha One and then some more outside of it. I don't want to be tied down. But I also don't know how to make her anything but disappointed in me.'

Lukas shook his head as if he could make the words less true. Katherine wished he had that power. There was a softness in his grey eyes that offered her comfort but also reflected no small amount of hurt. He stood so close to her that they were all she could look at. He blocked out the room, standing between her legs as close as it was possible.

'My parents' divorce was entirely my fault,' he said. 'If it weren't for me and my racing, my mother would never have left. I know that. And I know she blames me. I try to financially support her to make up for it but I know it's not enough. And when the divorce and my relationship with her became news, I was confronted with that every time I switched on the TV or went online. It's why I can't let the media in. Because then people would see how selfish I am, that I sacrificed my father's happiness for my own gain. I'd rather stay private so no one else has to know that but me and my mother.'

Katherine brought her hand up to touch his cheek and her heart soared at his infinitesimal lean into her caress. She'd bared a part of her soul to Lukas and he didn't judge. He didn't offer unsolicited advice or tell her she was wrong.

He'd shown her that he understood what a complicated relationship with a parent was like. That he saw her vulnerability and offered a piece of his own.

And now she understood why he hated the media so much. They didn't often look at him like a human. He was a celebrity. A public commodity for them to pry into and he was afraid that people would see him like he saw himself. They both had proud fathers and disapproving mothers, and she had to admit, she would hate for people to uncover that about her. It would hurt every time someone spoke about it.

Katherine realised how different the real Lukas was to the person the media portrayed him to be. She liked this man.

She kissed him softly on his lips. Her body tingled at the connection.

'Lukas,' she breathed and was met with a ferocious kiss. A kiss that made her mind go blank and her body light up like a Christmas tree.

'I have to confess something,' he said in between kisses. 'That day three years ago in the paddock, I thought you were the most beautiful woman I had ever seen. I walked away because I didn't want to talk to you. I didn't want to hear your voice or risk being charmed by you. I'd just had a relationship fail despite how much we loved each other, because I was so set on every part of it being in private. I couldn't be attracted to you when I was in a bad place. When you were the last person on earth I would ever consider being with.'

She rested her forehead against his. 'Because I'm a journalist.'

'The media has never been my friend, Katherine. I don't

need the world prying into my life, analysing everything about me.'

They were so different. Wanted different things. Trusted different people. And as long as she was a journalist he would never trust her.

And she was never going to sacrifice her career for anyone. Least of all him.

'I don't know why you're so against the world getting to know you, Lukas. Everything I see makes me want to know you even more. Everything I uncover blows me away. I'm glad we got stuck here. I'm glad I'm getting to know you like this. You're extraordinary, why do you want to hide? You're not the one who needs to feel guilty or apologise, but your mother should. She owes you an apology.'

'That's not why I'm telling you this.' He cupped her face, urging her to listen carefully. 'I can't be with you, Katherine. I value my privacy too much, that won't change. I gave up on a relationship because of the media, and after losing her, I won't enter into another relationship while I'm in the spotlight. Your career will always be in the way, but you're a drug and I'm addicted to you.'

He was right, on both counts. Their chemistry wouldn't be ignored. 'So we can have this time. Just until we're rescued and after that…'

'I'll go back to my life and you go back to yours,' he said.

So for now, she could just pretend.

Pretend as if everything was perfect so she could enjoy their chemistry. The pleasure. It would be a momentary distraction.

'I like the sound of that.'

The words barely left her mouth when Lukas lifted her and placed her on the pool table. A sudden rush of cool air

greeted her most intimate skin and she watched him kneel in front of her. His eyes glinting wickedly as his mouth closed over her core. Feasting on her like a starving man.
She could definitely agree to their terms for this.

CHAPTER NINE

WATER RAINED OVER Lukas and Katherine. Steam billowing around them in the ultra-luxurious bathroom.

He held Katherine to him. His talented fingers playing a melody of moans as if she were his favourite instrument. Each string he plucked had her bowing and arching against him. It was the sweetest music. The very best dance.

Every morning since their talk had started like this. Every moment since he'd tasted her on that pool table, he had craved her more and more and to his great delight, the feeling had been mutual.

Unable to keep their hands off each other, the days had blurred together. Lukas hadn't even minded that, after the brief moment when the skies cleared enough to see the aurora, they were back to wind and snow.

Until that morning.

They had awoken to blue skies. It was so bright with the blanket of snow magnifying the sunlight. The clear sky looked vivid, as if someone had painted it. And good weather meant rescue.

Their time was up.

Lukas was determined to enjoy what little they had left. And he had been enjoying their time. Once he understood why Katherine hated him, it was only natural that he should apologise because he still wanted her to do the same. He had endangered her dream, and her articles had endangered his.

So, he understood and welcomed the fact that this attraction had no chance of a future, but God, did he want to revel in this passion some more.

'Turn around,' he instructed, high on the fact that she obeyed him so readily. He wrapped an arm around her waist, holding her to him, and kissed her fiercely while turning off the taps. Bodies dripping, he picked her up and stepped out of the shower, then heard the unmistakable roar of a helicopter overhead.

'I think help is here,' Katherine whispered. Her lips pink and full from his kisses.

'We should get dressed,' he replied but made no move to put her down.

He watched her stare into his eyes. So much passing between them. Electricity, regret, passion but the thwop thwop of the rotors only got louder and louder.

'Put me down, Lukas.'

Clutching her tighter at first, he forced his muscles to relax and then set her on her feet. He turned away from her, dried off as fast he could and dressed in the clothes close at hand.

He ran his fingers through his hair and turned to look at Katherine, unsure of what he should say. What he could say. Maybe it was best he said nothing.

He rushed to the lounge, just in time to see Dominic force his way through the door.

'Lukas.'

He had never heard his manager, his friend, sound so relieved or look older than he did right then.

He watched Dominic stride through the room and Lukas embraced him tightly.

'I told them you would be fine,' Dominic said, voice muffled. 'I made them start here.'

Lukas chuckled as he pulled away. 'You weren't worried at all.'

'Bastard,' Dominic grumbled.

'Thank you,' Lukas said with as much gratitude as he could muster.

'For knowing you so well or coming to get you?'

'Both.' Lukas smiled. He turned in time to see Katherine enter the room, her bag rolling along behind her. He noticed once again that she was in the cameraman's jacket. He wanted so badly to march over to her and rip the jacket off her. To wrap her in his own and claim her, but that would go against what they had. A momentary flirtation in private while they were snowbound. If he showed any interest in her now, rumours about them would get out and spread like wildfire. If a relationship he had been so committed to had ended because he was unwilling to budge on his privacy, he couldn't go against his principles for a tryst. So he clenched his hands into fists and stayed where he was.

Katherine noticed. He could tell by her slightly cocked head.

'Katherine!' Dominic exclaimed with surprise. His eyes growing wide when he noticed her. 'How did you... We thought you were...' He looked back and forth between Lukas and her. 'Did you two get trapped together?'

'Yes,' she replied, coming closer. Lukas could feel the distance between them closing as if she was hooked onto a spool within him and when she joined them a mere foot away, it felt like she was an entire chasm away. He wanted to touch her. To hold her. To tell everyone to leave them alone for a few more weeks but he bit his tongue instead.

'Lukas saved me, actually. I hurt my ankle and he found me and then I wasn't surviving very well on my own so he brought me here.'

He ignored the impressed look on Dominic's face. He didn't want to acknowledge the hate that no longer existed between them or explain what the past week had been like.

'Thank heavens for Lukas.' Dominic squeezed her in a one-armed hug. 'I'm very glad you're okay, Katherine.'

'Thank you, Dominic.'

'Your crew will be returning shortly to pick up their stuff,' Dominic said, 'But how would you like to leave with us now?'

'I would love to.'

The helicopter ride from the cabin to Rovaniemi was uncomfortable. Lukas said nothing the entire flight but every time he looked at her she could feel the heat in his gaze. Her body reacted to him but no relief would come now. He wouldn't kiss her or take her to bed. All those touches lived only in her memory now. Katherine knew she would compare anyone in her future to Lukas and they would always fail in comparison. But they were over. They were rescued and it didn't matter that her heart was imploding for whatever ridiculous reason, they had an agreement.

As soon as they landed, she and Lukas were bundled into separate vehicles. She didn't even get the chance to say thank you or goodbye.

'*Hei*,' she greeted the driver. As soon as she buckled herself in she switched on her phone, which still had battery life having spent the week powered down in her suitcase. A series of vibrations went through her phone. One of them being an email with a plane ticket out of Rovaniemi Airport straight to Heathrow.

'Perfect.'

She closed her emails, wishing she could be home already. In those walls she could safely let herself miss Lukas. She could replay the night by the fireplace and think about how different a man he actually was to the one she reported about.

Like in the feature article she'd written. The things she'd said wouldn't reflect the man Lukas really was, so it wouldn't be true. She couldn't let it run after all he'd told her.

Katherine dialled her editor, drumming her fingers on the door-handle as she waited for her to pick up.

'Katherine! It's such a relief to hear your voice! I was so worried—'

'I need you to pull the feature,' she said.

'What?'

'Jennifer, I know what I'm asking and that feature on Lukas Jäger can't run. I'm begging you.' Her palms grew sweaty. Katherine had never once asked to pull a story before. 'I'll write something else in its place. Please.'

'Why?'

'I don't think it's true anymore.' Katherine scrunched her eyes shut, assaulted with images of Lukas talking to her, taking care of her, pleasuring her, cooking. But she couldn't say any of that. She forced herself to sound more in control. Rational. 'It doesn't accurately reflect who Lukas is.'

'It's a great piece though, Kat. What's brought on this change of heart?'

'Being stuck in a snowstorm.' Jennifer wasn't going to respond to an emotional appeal. The story came first so there was only one thing she could say to make her editor change her mind and agree. 'I've just had the opportunity no one else will ever have. Full access to Lukas Jäger. I've got to know the man behind the persona and if we print the article I first gave you, we wouldn't be printing the truth.'

'I'll see what I can do…but this means I want a new article covering what you've learnt about him or we'll come up with something else to get us those clicks.'

'Thanks, Jen.'

'You owe me,' her editor said and then added, 'I really am happy you're okay. You had us all worried there.'

'I'm okay. See you soon.'

Katherine never had a reason to doubt Jennifer Harrison, but somehow, she didn't feel reassured. Maybe she had grown a little protective of Lukas, but all she could do was hope Jennifer kept her word.

To distract herself, Katherine opened her socials. Going a week without checking in was alien to her and she needed to know what was going on. As soon as she opened the first app, she was greeted by thousands of notifications all tagging her and Lukas.

'What the…' She looked at a few of them, closed the app, opened another but it was the same. Another app…the same result. Thousands of posts covering her and Lukas missing in Lapland. That she'd expected, because Lukas had been right. With the way she had run off, that was what the crew would have reported. What she hadn't expected was the explosion of speculation about her relationship with Lukas. There were always posts like that, but this was different. #Lukat was trending on several sites. Theories ranged from the believable—that they got caught in a snowstorm—to the absurd—they'd deliberately run off before the storm to have a secret affair and being missing gave them uninterrupted time alone.

Would Lukas see this? How would he react?

She was still scrolling, unsure of how she felt about being the subject of internet speculation, when her phone rang.

'Hi, Robert,' she answered.

'It's good to know that you survived. Did Jäger?'

'If you're asking if I murdered him, I did not.' But it was a miracle she was alive with the number of times he'd robbed her of breath. Stopped her heart. Had her writhing and panting and begging.

'I'm very proud of you. The reason I called is that there's going to be a meeting tomorrow, at 10 a.m. Make sure you're there.'

'Shouldn't I be getting recovery time?' Recovery from her and Lukas's explosive fling. They shared so much in common but all they could ever have was years of hate followed by a week so unforgettable her last thought in this world would be of him.

'Kat, you've done nothing in that tundra. That's enough vacation time for you,' he joked. 'Tomorrow.'

'I'll be there.'

She ended the call with unease in her belly. Robert hadn't said what the meeting was about or who would be there. All she could do was turn up and hope nothing horrible had happened while she was gone.

Katherine walked into the glass-panelled conference room at the Aero offices with nothing but her computer, which she placed on the table, and took her seat. The same seat she always sat at. Back to the window that overlooked London with its steel-grey skies, old and new buildings standing proud on the banks of the Thames. It was a lovely view. A distracting one, which was why she never gave herself any other option than paying complete attention to the meeting. It also allowed her to see what was happening on the floor. Who entered the room even when the blinds were drawn. They weren't used often, only when absolute privacy was required. The room let out little to no sound and today, the blinds *were* drawn. Not an oversight from a previous meeting. She knew how this place operated.

It made her anxious.

Katherine had replayed Robert's short call in her mind repeatedly but there was nothing to analyse. He had given her nothing to go on so she gave up. Instead, she'd lain on her bed, staring at the ceiling…missing Lukas.

Why didn't I say goodbye? Why didn't I take one last kiss?

She had eventually fallen asleep, curled around the pillow, wishing it was his body. Regret her only companion.

Now she tried to push away thoughts of Lukas but there was no getting rid of them. Even as she watched Robert enter with Jennifer and Scott Courteney, a network executive she hadn't ever met. Though she was the on-air talent, he operated at a much higher level than her. So what was he doing here?

Suddenly that knot of anxiety grew into an entire noose.

'Katherine!' Robert greeted, coming around the table to give her shoulder a squeeze. 'It really is good to see you. I wasn't joking when I said you had us all worried.'

'It's a good thing I wasn't alone,' she replied, wincing internally at the stab of pain that thinking about Lukas brought about.

A look crossed her producer's face that she couldn't decipher. None of this was making her feel better.

'Absolutely. Have you met Scott before?'

'No, can't say I've had the pleasure.' She held out her hand, which Scott shook firmly but there was a glint in his eye that didn't sit well with her.

'Shall we take our seats?' Scott gestured at the table as he placed himself at the head. Robert took the seat next to her, closest to Scott and Jennifer sat on her other side, sandwiching her in. She didn't like it.

'Is anyone else coming?' Katherine asked.

'Yes, they should be along shortly,' Robert said.

That wasn't much information.

'What's this meeting about?' She tried a different tack.

'I'm sure you have plenty of questions, Ms Ward, but I think they can wait just a little longer.' Scott's clasped hands were placed on the table. A man so used to power that he had no problem telling her to be quiet. Because that was exactly what that sentence meant.

'Why don't you tell us what happened in Finland?' Robert suggested. Was he here just to be a buffer? To smooth over anything Scott might say to her?

Katherine had already rehearsed the story she would tell everyone. She knew it would come up again and again. Everyone was interested in Lukas and now people were interested in her too, but she didn't want the world to know about their tender moments. How they'd confided in each other about their mothers or just how much their careers meant to them because their fathers believed in them so much.

She told them everything but did well to leave out the intimate parts of her and Lukas's snowbound week. The parts that made her ache.

She noticed a look pass between the three of them. She was reaching the end of her patience. Whatever was going on was obviously linked to her adventure in Lapland; she had no idea what, but she was going to demand some answers. Just then the door opened and in walked Dominic Wilson, Lukas's manager, Erin Walker, his publicist and right behind them, there he was. Lukas in jeans, boots and a leather jacket. His eyes landed on her the moment he walked into the room and it was like all the air had been sucked out and at the same time she took her first real breath since they had gone their separate ways.

Was that really only yesterday?

He didn't stop looking at her even when Robert and Scott shook his hand. He didn't stop looking at her when he sat opposite her. An entire conference table between them but she wanted to crawl over the top of it to sit on his lap and kiss him. To hell with their agreement and everyone who was watching.

And she could see the heat fill his silver eyes when he read her thoughts.

Finally, he tore his gaze from hers and she saw it settle on Scott. The heat replaced by something icy. 'It's obvious you all have been planning something, so I suggest we get to the point.'

Katherine smiled inwardly. Lukas wasn't bound by the same behavioural expectations she was. He couldn't be fired for not showing the reverence someone like Scott expected. She wanted to mouth a thank you at him but instead sat quite still, waiting for all this secrecy to end.

'I think Robert should start,' Scott said and all eyes turned to the man sitting next to her.

He cleared his throat. 'Right. As we all know, there was some speculation about what happened to you both in Lapland. You were both on the news daily because there was no information about your well-being,' he said, glancing between her and Lukas. 'What we didn't expect was the level of speculation about the relationship between you two.'

Katherine got a sinking feeling in the pit of her stomach. Surely this wasn't heading where she thought it was.

'The public seemed largely to think that you two were an item or were going to be one and the level of interest that has generated can't be ignored.'

'Speak plainly,' Lukas ordered. His voice was growing lower. His brow furrowing.

Robert pulled some papers out of a folder in front of him that Katherine hadn't quite noticed before and handed them to everyone around the table. 'This is the increase in traffic to the Aero TV site since you two went viral.'

'We have seen similar impressions on Lukas's socials,' Erin added, and Lukas shot her a look that would have anyone shrinking. Katherine saw the apprehension on Erin's face but she pushed on. 'Here are some analytics on the Lukat hashtag.'

Katherine accepted the page from her but the words and infographics were blurring into one.

'This is why we've asked you two to be here today,' Jennifer said. She seemed as confident as always but, for the first time that day, Robert appeared nervous. 'This kind of attention is too great to ignore, so we think it would be best for you both to play into the rumours.'

This had gone exactly where Katherine feared.

'What?' Lukas growled.

There was no way Lukas was going to agree. She hadn't told anyone how they had connected, and she knew Lukas wouldn't have either. This was their secret. Something they had in private surrounded by a wall of snow. She didn't want to put themselves on display. Especially after they'd agreed on an end no matter how much her body and heart craved more.

Scott leaned forwards, placing his palm face down on the table, expecting everyone to give him their attention and everyone respectfully had, but Lukas looked at him with defiance.

He stared unwaveringly at the man and crossed his arms. Katherine couldn't imagine being more attracted to him than she was right now.

'No one is asking the world of either of you,' Scott said. 'You are both public figures. All that is expected is that you two pose as a couple for the next month and a half, which will bring us up roughly to the launch dates for next season's Alpha One cars. We will announce your break-up, and we'll have enough added interest to carry through testing and the season opener.'

'Entirely benefitting you,' Lukas sneered.

'It benefits everyone at this table.'

Lukas shook his head. His expression bored but Katherine knew better than that. He would be hating the very idea. His skin would be crawling. 'Absolutely not.'

'Lukas—' Robert started but Lukas cut him off.

'I will not have my private life splashed about the media like some performance,' Lukas spat. 'You are all entitled to my time on the track but away from it, none of you has any right to anything from me. This whole idea is ridiculous.'

Katherine tried not to take his vehemence personally but it still stung. Being together hadn't seemed ridiculous a day ago. But he was right. This idea didn't benefit her. She was only twenty-seven. She still had her whole career ahead of her. There was no guarantee that she would spend it all with Aero TV and if this ever got out, her career would be ruined. She'd done everything right from the moment she started school. Being the journalist she was didn't happen overnight. It had been a lifetime of working hard and now they wanted her to kiss and flirt with a man so they could increase their ratings. Make more money. But what about her integrity? Her reputation?

'What do you have to say?' Lukas asked her and all heads swivelled towards her. Encouragement on Jennifer's and Robert's faces, something hard on Scott's, curiosity on Dominic's and Erin's. But Lukas…he only expected an answer. Nothing more.

'I don't want to do it. It's too much of a risk to my career if it ever got out. It benefits everyone but me.'

'It benefits the network, Ms Ward,' Scott said.

'The higher ratings benefit you, Kat,' Robert said in a placating tone. 'Imagine how much further your name would go. Think about the clout you would have to negotiate your next contract.'

'Ms Ward.' Scott Courteney turned to face her. To intimidate her. 'You need to be a team player and do your part. We're all working to grow this network.'

'No.' Katherine refused to budge, and she could see pride in Lukas's eyes.

Scott's expression turned menacing. '*Kat*, do you want to work here?'

'What just a minute—' Lukas gritted out.

'You can't be serious,' Katherine spoke over him. She glanced at the man who just tried to stand up for her, who made butterflies take flight in her belly with just a look. Just a touch. And she saw pride had turned into glittering anger.

Jennifer swivelled her chair to face Katherine. 'We could always find other ways to maximise interest, but they wouldn't be as mutually beneficial. Articles we could run.'

Jennifer's gaze bored into her own and a shiver passed down Katherine's spine. She would run the feature article despite being asked not to. Despite the fact that it wasn't true. But if everyone already thought Katherine and Lukas had been together in Lapland and an article came out that was written by her attacking him, the world would tune in for the drama. She would get a reputation for being unscrupulously ruthless and Lukas would lose any opportunities he had left. She couldn't do that to him. Do that to herself.

'The visibility will definitely be good for *both* of you,' Erin said, trying to diffuse the situation, but it didn't matter because Katherine was backed into a corner. Either she said yes or she lost her job, her reputation, Lukas's career. She'd worked too hard for all that she had achieved for it all to fall apart now. Scott would fire her and hire some other new face who was passionate about the sport. This was her dream career. And what if she said no and lost it all but Lukas's PR team still used the idea as a Hail Mary and forced him to go with it—because she knew how much his career meant to him? Would they find someone else to agree to this ridiculousness?

Some other woman who would get to be with him and touch him and listen to his voice and that accent she now found so endearing.

She hated the idea.

So here she was. She could agree or lose her job because of a situation with Lukas.

It's not his fault.

No, it wasn't but Katherine couldn't refuse. It would cost her her career and she would not let Lukas jeopardise her job again. Never again.

'Fine, I'll do it,' she said, defeat clear in her voice to all at the table.

* * *

Lukas wanted so badly to be angry at Katherine for agree-ing. It had felt like they were on the same page in their op-position to this ludicrous proposition and it had felt good. Like maybe in this small way they could be a team. Be something more than the nothing they were forced to be by going back to their own lives now that they had left Finland. But he couldn't blame her. He knew what this job meant to her and this asshole threatening her career had Lukas seeing red.

Maybe it was good she had agreed because they wouldn't be able to blame her when he refused and brought this madness to a halt.

'But I won't be.'

'Lukas—' Dominic finally spoke up '—listen to them.'

He had never been more furious at his manager than right now.

'We are all aware of your current predicament in the sport, Lukas,' Scott said in a way that he clearly thought was charming, but really, all it did was make him come off as slimy. 'This is your last shot.'

'We're all working to leverage this attention for both of you,' Erin said. 'Despite the negative publicity that initially made them nervous—' she glanced briefly at Katherine '—teams would take you over someone in their academy or a pay-to-drive racer if they can get some sort of ROI with you. With all this attention, you would be bankable. You'd attract sponsors for the team. Your name would be worth even more money than it already is.'

Pay-to-drive. ROI. It was all so money dependent now. Where did talent lie? Lukas was confident he could take any car farther up the field than any of the teams still needing drivers could currently imagine being, but he was forced to consider how he could make them money away from the track too. As if championship winnings were no longer enough. It made white-hot heat fill his body. Blood pound in his ears.

'Lukas,' Dominic said. He knew the tone well. It was usually followed by something blunt he didn't want to hear. 'Do you want to have a drive next year? I'm doing all that I can. Erin and I both are. We wouldn't be sitting here if we didn't think this was your best option. There are two teams who haven't signed a second driver and at this point I'd say they are 75 to 80 percent more likely to sign two rookies. But we are trying our best to shift the needle here. Trying to get them to look at you as their saving grace, because we know you can be the difference between them earning sixty million or eighty million dollars.'

Those numbers meant that Lukas's options were firmly at the back of the grid, but at least he would be racing. If he could get the teams more sponsorships that meant more money and better car development, so maybe they would be able to fight even higher than that. But it would also mean that his privacy went out the window. That people could see who he was. That maybe they would see the boy who chose himself and imploded his parents' happiness for his own selfish reasons.

It occurred to him that if he took the team principal job he wouldn't have to deal with any of this nonsense. But he wouldn't be racing. All the sacrifice would have been for nothing. How could he have cost his father so much, only to see the dream die now? He owed his father.

He had to drive.

He pinched the bridge of his nose. How awful would agreeing be?

'Lukas?' He was giving Katherine his attention before

he had even realised that it was her voice that called him. He wanted so badly to kick everyone out of this room and take her on the table. Show her how crazy he had been going since they got into that helicopter yesterday. This woman who was intelligent and beautiful. And who had just had her career threatened. If he said no, would he be jeopardising her career again? He knew how much it meant to her, because he knew how much his own meant to him. Their reasons were so similar.

Instead of hurting her he could help her.

And he could have a month with her. Extend the pleasure a little longer.

Yes.

His body cried out.

'I'll do it.' He was nauseous.

'Great,' Robert said but Lukas wasn't looking at him. Not at any of them, but Katherine. 'So now you will leave with Kat out the front of the building.'

'Yes, that will result in pictures on the internet for sure,' Erin agreed. 'It's best that we waste no time.'

'We have photographers stationed strategically as well to ensure there are a number of them,' Jennifer informed them.

'Enough.' Lukas brought his hand down on the glass table making everyone flinch. 'I've agreed to your plan but that's all you're getting out of me. None of you get to dictate anything further to me or to Katherine, am I clear?'

'Be reasonable,' Robert pleaded.

'All of you get out,' Lukas said to the others.

'Lukas…' He heard Scott's voice. The disapproval that he couldn't give a damn about.

He looked only at Katherine. 'I said get out. Leave us.'

He heard the shuffling. The footsteps. The snick of the

door shutting. Once they were alone he got out of his chair and went to Katherine, taking her hand and making her stand before him.

The urge to touch her was too great, he couldn't stop himself from running his hand up her arm, over her shoulder, cupping her cheek. His thumb caressed her porcelain skin.

Are you okay? he wanted to ask. *Are you sure you want to do this because I don't,* he wanted to say, but he didn't. He couldn't. The future of their careers was hanging over their heads. What choice did either of them have if they wanted to hold on to their dreams?

Katherine seemed to understand what he wanted to say.

'It won't be forever,' she whispered.

'It won't.' But it felt like they were talking about so much more than this plan. They had another chance to be together. Weeks this time. Hours and hours to indulge the chemistry that was still so potent Lukas had to fight to stop himself kissing her here. But he would have to kiss her, and there would be pictures. His life that he had worked so tirelessly to keep private would be advertised for the world to see.

How could one person want something so badly and so utterly hate how they were getting it?

He was selling out his principles to keep his racing career alive. For a bit of time with Katherine. His father had always taught him to stand up for his beliefs, but he'd caved. What would he think of Lukas if he could see him now?

CHAPTER TEN

LUKAS SAT OPPOSITE Katherine in his private jet. She had said very little since they had left Aero. In fact, when he had said they would be travelling to Monaco to spend the time there, she had put up very little fight. Instead, she had seemed lost in thought.

That was fine. Once they got to his home, they would have the privacy they needed to talk. So for now, he gave her the space she needed.

Not that much space.

His jet had eight leather seats. Plus, he had a bedroom at the back of the plane hidden behind a polished wall. He could have sat anywhere else, but he didn't want to. He wanted to be around Katherine. Needed to be close to her. She didn't bring him peace. No. She made him feel like he was attached to a live wire. She focussed all his attention on her. Consumed him. And *that* was as close to peace as he got.

He led her by the hand to the waiting helicopter that would fly them to Monaco when they landed in Nice. Even while they buckled themselves in, he didn't let go. He didn't want to. It was only a seven-minute flight but with her hand in his and their shoulders brushing, Lukas was thrown into a dimension where every minute dragged for hours and yet somehow, he hadn't realised they had landed until the doors opened.

He needed to get home. Needed a moment with her in private to kiss her. To talk to her. To find a boundary he could work with, because right now he couldn't think clearly.

As soon as they stepped into his apartment Lukas could breathe again. Tension that had bunched his muscles from the moment they were rescued ebbed away. Here, he could be himself. There was no one watching, no one to judge him.

No one to support you. No one to be happy you've returned.

He was always greeted with silence.

'Lukas?'

Except today.

'I'll show you to your room. We can talk after,' he said, leading her through the entrance to his three-storey apartment. An apartment that was filled with so much light even though the sky was overcast and a drizzle fell as far as the eye could see.

'No,' Katherine refused, halting her steps and bringing her bag to a stop beside her. 'I want to talk first.'

'Fine. Come with me,' he said, placing his hand on the small of her back and leading her forward. 'Leave your bag. I'll take it up to your room.'

He took her into a lounge area with large overstuffed couches and a double height ceiling. A balcony to another floor wrapped around the square with tall narrow gold square poles placed in irregular intervals like a crown if a room could ever have one.

'We're just over two weeks into December and you have no Christmas decorations up.'

'I don't see the point of celebrating a holiday that does nothing but show me that I have no family to spend it with.' Lukas tried to keep his voice as emotionless as possible. He missed his father every day; he didn't need a holiday to make that worse. And his mother? Well, he understood her not wanting to see the reason her marriage failed.

'Have a seat.' When she obeyed, he sat on the coffee table in front of her. 'Do you want to go first?'

She didn't hesitate. 'Why did you bring me here? I'm still a journalist, Lukas. Nothing's changed.'

'You're right, nothing has changed and yet everything has.' Lukas leaned forward, clasping his hands between his knees to stop himself reaching for Katherine. They needed to establish rules before he allowed himself the pleasure. A pleasure he'd been robbed of since their rescue. One that he craved so badly he was currently leaving crescent-shaped indents on the back of his hands. 'I don't want to invite the media into my home and I'm *not* doing so. Understand that, Katherine. Whatever happens within these walls is not for a report. *But* it was best to come here. It's where I am comfortable. Where we can both be comfortable and have space should we need it. It's a place where we don't have to pretend, but when we step outside…'

'The cameras will go off,' Katherine finished for him. 'Monaco is small enough that it would take minutes to come back here should we need sanctuary.'

Lukas nodded, glad that she understood. 'There's enough space for you to work and you're free to use all the facilities in my home.'

'Thank you. But you still haven't addressed *us*.'

That's when Lukas noticed her hands. Fingers fidgeting with a ring. She needed to know where they stood just as much as he did.

He placed his large hand over hers. 'We're in this position because we had very few options and if it wasn't for that meeting we would have been over.'

'Does that mean you want us to remain that way? Over?' Katherine asked, her hands wrapping around his.

'We don't have a future. We're too different in the ways that matter.' Katherine slowly pulled her hands from his but he wouldn't let her. 'But I would be lying if I said that I want us to be a thing of the past. I'm giving you the choice, Katherine, because if it were up to me, you would be in my bed already. You would have barely made it into this apartment before I ravaged your lips and had your body against mine. Any second now you would have been screaming out my name but no one would have heard you. No one would have seen you and not because we were forced into a cabin in the middle of nowhere, but because we chose to take the privacy we're owed.'

'So you still want me.'

'I wanted you the very first time I saw you. That's never changed.' Lukas pulled Katherine off the couch to straddle his lap. She ran her fingers through his hair, tugging it back; he looked into the depths of her blue eyes made all the more vivid by her red lashes. 'Do you know how frustrating it is to be so attracted to the person you hate. Who you know hates you?'

'Do you still hate me?' she whispered so close to his lips that her breath tickled his skin.

'No.'

She smiled. 'I don't hate you either.'

And then he kissed her.

CHAPTER ELEVEN

KATHERINE AWOKE TO bright sunshine in a large, spectacularly appointed room with gold and marble accents. Monaco and the Mediterranean Sea lay beyond the windows, which had no treatments to distract from the view. She levered herself onto her elbows. Despite it being December, she saw plenty of people on the water in their yachts.

Never in her wildest dreams had she ever thought she would be in this position. Living in a driver's home, pretending to be in a relationship with him. *Pretending* was the important part. That's why after enjoying Lukas's passion in the lounge, she'd asked to be taken to her room.

This wasn't a real relationship. They were doing this because they were backed into a corner and neither of them wanted to risk their careers. Anything more than that was simply an opportunity to indulge in some pleasure, but pleasure was all it was. Katherine didn't want a relationship with anyone. She didn't want to move in with anyone. Love was dangerous. Love derailed dreams and then what would she be left with? A life of mediocrity and unfulfillment while trying to convince herself that she was just fine? No, thanks.

She wasn't her mother. Katherine wouldn't let that happen to her.

But thoughts of her mother made her realise that her parents would have been unprepared for the wave of news announcing her relationship with Lukas. Last time she'd spoken to them she was assuring them that she'd never been in any danger in Lapland. That there was no truth to the rumours, and she'd promised to visit the first chance she got.

Katherine groaned and flopped back on the pillows.

She reached for her phone and just as she expected there were numerous calls and messages from both her parents. Well, only one from her father—the only one that made her feel guilty.

Why didn't you tell us? You didn't have to hide it. Take care of yourself, Kittykat. Enjoy Monaco.

He loved the sunshine, would love it here.

Isn't it a pity that he'll never meet Lukas?

Yes. No. It wasn't a real relationship, so no, it wasn't a pity.

I have no family to spend it with.

Her father would never let Lukas feel so alone. He didn't let her feel alone.

For twenty weekends in a year, that was.

'No! Stop it, Katherine,' she ordered herself and got out of bed. Her phone lighting up as she did so.

It was a message from Robert.

Scott isn't happy that you two are hiding out in Monaco. I suggest getting out for some 'in public' time.

Scott Courteney being unhappy wasn't a good thing for her, so Katherine went down to the lower level—she had found out it contained the kitchen, two dining areas, a lounge and a home theatre, which was a lot of space to entertain for a man so alone—barefoot in her satin pyjamas. The aroma of freshly brewed coffee led her to the kitchen where Lukas was shirtless and sweaty in a pair of grey track pants hanging low on his hips, downing a bottle of water. Drop after drop of perspiration ran down his carved torso to the band of his pants where they were wicked by the fabric. Heat rushed to Katherine's face. A tightening in her core.

'Good morning.' There was a teasing lilt to his voice. Obviously he'd caught her staring. She did that a lot but honestly, how could she not when he looked like a fantasy given life?

'Would you like some coffee? I don't have any tea. I wasn't expecting guests.'

'Do you ever?' She walked up to him and curled her hands in the fabric of his pants, giving him the smallest of kisses, growing satisfied at his gasp. It was only fair to level the playing field.

'Not in recent years,' he admitted.

How lonely.

'I have a life, Katherine. I just don't like bringing the world into my sanctuary.'

'But you brought me here.'

'I did.' He said nothing else. Instead, he reached for a cup and poured her a coffee. It wasn't how she normally started her day, but she had always loved coffee. She developed the habit of drinking tea because that was what everyone else in her home preferred growing up and she didn't want to be demanding, so she had made do. Now starting her day with a cup of tea was habit.

'Robert messaged me, they want us to go out in public today.' She sipped the coffee, relishing the comforting warmth. It wasn't overly bitter, and she could taste notes of dark chocolate and caramel. It was delicious.

'I expected as much. It's a good thing I already had a plan, then, isn't it?'

'Oh? And what's that?'

'Get dressed and I'll show you.'

Lukas's plan was strutting down a street. Maybe that wasn't completely fair. They walked hand in hand down the most high-end street in Carré d'Or. Haute couture brands lined up everywhere she looked. Lukas had taken her shopping—a normally mundane outing yet with him it was anything but. Her heart hadn't found a steady rhythm since he'd held her hand. It was made even worse by the kiss he had given her outside a world-famous bag boutique that had rendered her light-headed. From one store to the next he had spoilt her. Something that wasn't spoken about in their agreement, but she had also never seen him in such a good mood and it made her wonder if he enjoyed taking care of people.

Hadn't he said he wanted to do so for his mother? But his mother didn't want to see him. Katherine moved closer to him, and he slipped his hand from hers, wrapping it around her shoulders.

Not real.

She had to keep reminding herself of that fact.

'You're quiet,' Lukas said, his dark sunglasses hooked on the front of his shirt.

'Aren't I always?'

The sound that came out of him was somewhere between a chuckle and a snort. It was the most undignified she had ever seen him and she had seen him use some colourful language on the team radio over the years. She couldn't help but laugh.

'Is that a no?'

'What is the saying you English use? When pigs fly?'

Katherine laughed harder then. He spoke so well that sometimes she forgot English wasn't his first language. She wiped a tear and saw a softness enter his eyes but he quickly looked away, so she did too.

'That jacket is stunning.' She tried to change the subject but it was clearly the wrong thing to say with Lukas being in such an odd mood, because he immediately led them inside.

'Try it on.'

'Lukas, it's really not necessary,' she tried to refuse.

Just then a very polished shop assistant came towards them. 'Can I help you?'

'No.'

'Yes.'

They said in unison.

'Yes,' Lukas insisted. 'She would like to try on that coat.' He pointed at the window.

'Of course, right this way.'

'You're being ridiculous,' Katherine whisper shouted.

'Am I, or are you?' Lukas challenged. 'How often do you get opportunities like this?'

Never, really. Katherine earned a very comfortable living and if everything went to plan it would only get better. That was why she was here, so that she didn't lose her career progress. So that she could eventually be rich and successful enough to take care of her parents. So that they could retire. And so that Paige, and to a lesser degree Christopher and Nicholas, would have a safety net. Buying a five-thousand euro coat wasn't on her radar. She had big-picture concerns.

'From the look on your face I'm going to say not often. So let me spoil you. You only have to put up with it for a month.'

Katherine hated the way that reminder made her mood plummet, but she forced herself to smile and said, 'Thank you.'

She went into the fitting room and tried the coat on. It was perfect. As if some magical tailor had made it to her exact measurements. She looked at the black fabric and white floral detail from every angle in the large cubicle fitted with the flattering light, and just as she slipped it off her shoulders and back on the hanger there was a knock on the door. She opened it a smidge and found Lukas on the other side holding a dress. Before she knew it, he was barging in and locking the door behind him.

'I want you to wear this.'

'What?'

'Try it on.'

'You realise you've walked into my fitting room, right?' The audacity of this man, barging his way in and making demands.

'Yes, I'm aware. I know I drive on a closed track, but I have a very good sense of direction.'

'You're impossible.'

He simply shrugged.

'Are you leaving?'

'Would you mind if I stayed?'

'No.' She really didn't. She loved the way he didn't hide his attraction to her, and how it made her feel. Was this appropriate in such an exclusive store? Katherine found that she didn't much care.

She took off her sweater and her jeans while looking at Lukas, whose grey eyes had darkened like a storm. Still, she watched him watching her as she slipped on the soft, heavy dress. The weight made sense since it was covered in sequins. The softness was surprising.

'Turn around.'

She obeyed and saw herself and Lukas reflected at her. Could see when he bent, trailing kisses up her spine as he pulled the zip all the way up.

'Beautiful.'

This dress was more than just beautiful. The long sleeves sat off her shoulders. From chest to toes she was covered in glittering sequins forming a silver and gold gradient. It fit every curve until her hips where it flared out just slightly in a sparkling column.

'Look at me.'

Her eyes found his in the mirror, watching him trail kisses over her shoulder, along her neck. His hands gliding down her covered arms to her waist and then he spun her around, pushing her against the mirror. Her chest heaving even though he hadn't done very much. But then his nose was running along her neck. His lips brushing after.

'You'll wear this tomorrow,' he said. Instructed.

'Why?'

'That's not what you should be saying.' He inched the dress up higher and higher, gathering the fabric of the skirt in his hands, allowing one of them to trail over the inside of her thigh until he reached her sex covered in satin and lace, and he hummed in approval.

'You should be saying, "Yes, Lukas."'

She could hear his smirk but couldn't look because his fingers were taking her apart and putting her back together.

'Lukas,' she breathed.

He chuckled, deep and low. 'That's half right.'

She couldn't think when a moan was building in her throat.

'Quiet,' he said, then he kissed her deeply, swallowing every sound she made as his fingers drove her to insanity. Her hips meeting the movement of his skilled hand, wanting, needing more.

'You're being so good for me right now,' he praised. His lips brushing hers as he said the words. The taunt of a kiss and it was all too much. His words and fingers and lips, and then his tongue was in her mouth silencing her as she climaxed in a fitting room in Monaco wearing the most expensive dress she ever had on.

'Yes, Lukas,' she agreed because, if this was a taste of what awaited, she would wear anything to have more of him.

CHAPTER TWELVE

LUKAS WAS PULLING out all the stops. An all-black Bugatti waited in the portico of his building, the headlights switched on. Gleaming the way it did against the late dusk sky, the car seemed like some kind of spectre. Dark and mysterious.

If Robert and Scott wanted her and Lukas to be seen, they would certainly get their wish.

Katherine had done as Lukas asked and worn the incredible dress he'd bought her. Her stomach felt like she was in a rollercoaster every time she thought about what had occurred in the fitting room. No matter what happened after this month, she would keep this dress forever—a reminder of the racer she had been so wrong about. The man who brought her to life. The passion that was only bestowed upon a lucky few maybe once in a lifetime.

'Ready?' Lukas asked beside her.

She nodded. 'Yes.'

He took her hand, led her to the car and helped her in before closing the door and getting in himself. Something about this night felt different. It had felt different since they'd left the fitting room but Katherine couldn't quite put her finger on what it was.

Was it Lukas? Was he being more attentive? Or was it

her? Was it the way she felt about Lukas that was morphing into an affection she couldn't name?

She tried to pay little attention to what happened outside the car as Lukas drove the short distance to the Monte Carlo casino, but she couldn't not notice the number of phones in hands that followed them as they drove by, and when they reached the valet and exited Lukas's car.

Katherine was always on the other side of the media and now, just as Lukas was watched and snapped and recorded every moment he wasn't in his home, so was she. She wasn't sure she liked it all that much. Yes, she was in the public eye, but it was never, ever like this.

She felt Lukas's arm around her shoulders and gave him a small smile. She really hadn't appreciated his patience before.

'You look beautiful,' he said.

'Thank you.'

'Ignore them.'

Her steps slowed. 'What?'

'Keep walking and I said, "Ignore them."' His arm drew her tighter to him. More protectively. And when she looked up, there was a look in his eyes that took her breath away. 'The longer this goes on, the worse it's going to be. Cameras are going to follow you everywhere. The best thing you can do is ignore the attention.'

They reached the grand entrance to the casino where people the world over wished to visit but only a handful ever would. Lukas tilted Katherine's chin up and she gazed at his face. At the determined expression.

'And you can trust me to protect you.'

Katherine's throat went dry. Had he really noticed her discomfort with the attention she received? Attention was something she craved but never asked for. Now she was getting it in spades, so why was it bothering her?

'I—'

'Can protect yourself? I know you can, but this is something you're unprepared for. This kind of attention is invasive. It's not curious; it's entitled.'

'How did you...' Katherine wasn't sure what she was asking. *How did he know? What was he really saying?*

'There was attention that I craved and never received too, Katherine, but I knew this—' he tilted his head in the direction of flashing cameras '—wasn't it.'

Lukas understood her like no one else. If they stood out here any longer, the world would witness her getting emotional and she didn't want them to see her like that. Never mind that such a display would get the tabloids going crazy, because that was the unfortunate side effect of playing it up for Aero TV. The tabloids were having a field day.

'I think we should go inside.'

He smiled. 'That is probably a good idea.'

'So we're gambling tonight,' Katherine said in a light tone she forced when they climbed the stairs and walked through the historic doors.

'No.'

'Okay...then what are we doing at a casino?'

'Being seen and not heard.' His smile held a secret.

'You know what, I'm not even going to ask. Lead the way.'

Lukas noticed Katherine struggling with being in the public eye at this level. This wasn't anything like her job and he knew how violating it felt. Yes, she'd agreed to this, but it didn't mean she deserved to feel that way. He could help her. Was helping her. He was protecting her by bringing her into his home, taking her shopping where they would have constant reprieves whenever they went into the high-end stores, and bringing her here where the clientele was so exclusive. And that was why he took her into a restaurant.

'*Bonsoir*,' an elegant hostess greeted. '*Bienvenue*. Your table is waiting, Mr Jäger. Please follow me.'

Lukas placed his arm around Katherine's waist, holding her close as they followed the hostess through the stunning frescoed restaurant and into a cozy private corner near a window. The tables around them were empty. A reserved sign on each of them.

He held the chair out for Katherine and once she was seated, rounded the table to his own. The hostess handed them menus and left.

'Did you reserve all these tables?' Katherine asked. 'Is that how you made sure we wouldn't be heard?'

'I'm a selfish man, Katherine. I want your attention focussed solely on me.' A lie it was more convenient to tell, because the truth was that he wanted to spend all the time he could with her alone. He wanted her smiles and her candid honesty and her passion. He wanted them to be trapped in a bubble where he could lavish his attention on her and in return she would wholly want him. But wanting that much was a secret because she was only with him to save her career and enjoy some no-strings sex.

'I don't think that's true,' she said, leaning towards him. 'I don't think you're selfish. I think you were made to feel that way but really, you're generous and kind and protective.'

'Is that so?' He didn't want to say more than that and give away how he felt to have someone see him that way. He had never spoken to his father about his feelings regarding his parents' divorce or his mother's disapproval.

He had never wanted his father to be forced to comfort him and lie to him. To tell him that his mother was wrong. It would have hurt his father to say that. It was better to be the son his father needed him to be.

'Yes.' She reached across the table and placed her hand on his. A burning, sparking touch he wanted pressed against his cheek, a comfort he wanted to soak up. 'And I truly don't understand how you've been single for so long or why.'

Because his choices had consequences, that was why. And he couldn't put another person through the way he lived his life.

A waiter approached the table and Lukas gestured to Katherine to order, all the while watching her. The way she smiled and laughed and bantered. The way her red hair glowed under the lights. The way the gleam from the candle on the table sparkled in her blue eyes. She was incredible. So full of life and determination. She was also the only person he had met who he could relate to.

'And for you, monsieur?'

'I'll have the same and a glass of your best Bordeaux for Ms Ward.'

'Of course.'

'You knew I liked red wine?' Katherine asked when the waiter left and Lukas was forced to show just how much attention he'd paid to her over the years.

'There was a discussion about wine between you, and some of the drivers when we were in France once. You mentioned a Bordeaux you tried—'

Her eyes grew wide. 'That I loved... Lukas, that was two years ago. You weren't even there.'

'I wasn't part of your conversation, but I was there. I watched and listened,' he confessed and then made another confession. 'And to answer your previous question, I've been single this long because of choices I made.'

Katherine's frown was a silent request for him to continue.

'I was in a relationship for two years. We lived together. I was certain I would marry her. I loved her and in my mind we were already committed to growing old together.'

'What!' The surprise on her face was almost comical. 'I had no idea.'

'No one did, and that was the problem. No one knew because I was determined to maintain our privacy. Protect us from the press and scrutiny. But keeping it hidden forced us to be so careful of what we did and where we went. Whether people would take pictures of us. We tried to be happy, but she grew tired of how viciously I protected our privacy.'

You're snuffing out the life in me, Lukas. I want to have fun. Not be sequestered in the shadows so no one ever sees us, or takes a picture of us. I won't wait for you to be ready to live. You need to figure this thing out with the media because they are never going away, but I am.

'She said she couldn't live like that. As if we were sneaking around doing something wrong.'

Katherine was quiet, listening and not interrupting. He could see her curiosity and a part of him wondered if he was being stupid, telling her something so private. She was still a journalist and only on this date because that career in the media had been threatened. But something in him wanted to keep talking to her, so he did.

'I thought we could just deal with the years I had to be in the spotlight and once I retired we could finally have the life we wanted and things would get better. But I was wrong. She was right to leave because I was being selfish again. *I* didn't want our relationship in the media, so I forced that on her without considering what she wanted. She said she just wanted to be able to live her life. It wasn't a great time,' he said, looking out the window at the sparkling lights of Monaco, certain that he saw a few flashes go off in the distance. 'Two weeks later we were at the season opener and I saw you,' he looked at Katherine then, remembering the way his steps had come to an abrupt halt when he'd seen her. She had taken his breath away. That attraction had never waned. Sitting here with her in that sparkling dress, it was stronger than ever. It had just magnified after getting a taste of her.

She laughed but it was sad. 'You saw me and were attracted to me and everything went to hell.'

'Yes,' he agreed. 'I decided after that it would be best for me to be alone until I retired.' He saw the waiter approaching and leaned back in his chair. Katherine followed his movements. They kept silent while their meal was placed in front of them then thanked the server and waited for them to leave. Only then did they resume their conversation.

'I don't understand something,' Katherine said. 'If driving hurts you so much at this point, why are you so adamant about continuing? I know what you said about your father, but how is this for you? You're the one who has to live with this career.'

'I don't have to. I have another option.' The words were out of his mouth before he could stop them, but now he wanted to tell Katherine. No one knew. Not even Dominic. 'I have an offer on the table from Vortex Racing.'

'Not to drive, obviously.' Because they already had a confirmed driver line-up.

'To be their team principal.'

'Wow,' Katherine breathed, sitting back in her chair. 'That's huge! But if you're still looking for a drive, that means you turned them down?'

'I haven't given them an answer,' Lukas admitted, picking up his fork, but all he did was push the food around his plate.

'This is a massive opportunity, Lukas.' Katherine sat up straighter, a small frown creasing her forehead as she placed her palms on the table. This was analytical Katherine. The side of her that absorbed information and made connections from it, and it was fascinating to watch.

'Okay, so they're new and unlikely to be very competitive in their first year. Their factory is small but they have attracted some big talent behind the scenes so I think they will have one of the better designed cars, which means there's potential even with them having a customer engine. With your name attached, more sponsors would invest and that could make a difference. Just your name attached...' She looked at Lukas and he stopped breathing, but it didn't stop him from listening to her. 'But with you leading the team, Lukas, I'd say two maybe three years at a push before that car's winning races.'

He placed his fork down on his plate. 'I don't know, Katherine. I don't know if I'm ready to leave the cockpit. If I'm ready to lead a team,' he admitted.

'You have already led a team as a driver. You have so much knowledge...such an understanding of the car and the craft that even from a technical aspect you could make a difference. Then there's the fact that you took Dudek's team from nowhere to a championship. You've done it with two different teams. If there's anyone who knows how to win a championship, it's you.'

'But it isn't driving.'

She leaned towards him, placing her elbows on the linen tablecloth and shaking her head. 'No, it isn't, but is driving what you're really passionate about?' she asked intensely.

Lukas couldn't answer that. He loved driving but he couldn't honestly say that he was as passionate about it now as he used to be. He was jaded.

'From where I'm sitting, driving is keeping you in this weird purgatory where your life is on hold. You're alone because of it. And you don't have to be alone, Lukas.'

'I could say the same thing about you.' He needed to move the conversation away from this topic because Katherine was starting to make more sense than he wanted to hear.

'That's different,' she said softly, picking up her utensils.

'Why? You are not your mother. You have achieved so much more than everyone else in your family has. Why are you letting your mother's choices warn you away from a possible future?' It was an invasive question, Lukas knew, but he wanted to understand everything about Katherine. He needed to.

'My achievements so far are precisely why I won't let myself fall in love. It's proof of what I can have without that distraction. Without the risk of having or wanting to give everything up for one person. I have responsibilities.'

'Tell me about them.'

She placed her knife down and picked at the duck on her plate with her fork. 'My parents are getting older and will soon have to retire, but that won't be possible if Paige keeps getting into trouble. One time it was shoplifting, another it was drugs. There's always something. She can't hold down a job. One time she decided on a whim to pawn a bunch of things and flew to Europe where she worked odd jobs to move around between countries until she ran out of money and my dad had to go and get her.'

'Did he miss something important?' Lukas guessed he must have. If Paige caused disaster after disaster, not every mistake would be remembered, but the ones that hurt in some way would.

'A celebration dinner when I got my very first media job. It was the first step in our plan and I knew he wanted to celebrate with me but he couldn't. I understood, but it still hurt.'

'You didn't have to be understanding. He could have made her wait. He could have sent her the money to get back and whatever happened after that would have been her choice as an adult,' Lukas argued, but Katherine's family history was starting to become so clear.

'I did have to. I'd vowed to be the one they never had to worry about. And that's why I have to be a success, Lukas. Because if I have the resources to take care of Paige, then my parents can enjoy their golden years. And then I'll have to care for them. Someone will have to pay for facilities they'll need later in life. Someone will have to cover for all the savings they lost on rescuing my siblings. And besides all of that, this sport is my life. It's my dream. I can't lose it. Not for anyone or anything.'

'I'm sorry, Katherine. I didn't realise just how much I jeopardised by speaking so carelessly back then. In your place I would have hated me too.'

'I'm sorry I didn't give you the chance to explain. Maybe we could have had this sooner.'

Lukas didn't care who was watching then, he leaned across the table and kissed Katherine bruisingly, wishing for the same. Wishing for more. Wishing that he had done a better job guarding his heart against her, because this affection for a woman he could never have hurt him more than hating her ever did.

CHAPTER THIRTEEN

KATHERINE WORKED QUICKLY and quietly to put the finishing touches on the Christmas decorations that now hung in the lounge.

After their dinner—and after that kiss that had felt so real her heart had started pounding in panic and exhilaration—they had returned home and Lukas had gone to his room and stayed there. When she'd come down for breakfast that morning, there had been no sign that he'd woken or worked out, which had been odd. But it had been an opportunity.

Katherine was now getting to experience what life was like for Lukas. Alpha One was his whole life, but there was so much that shouldn't have to come along with it, which he was navigating the best he could. The unwanted attention, the loneliness. And he was lonely.

A holiday that does nothing but show me that I have no family to spend it with.

Lukas was caring and supportive and generous and kind. He had been proving that to her over and over. Taking care of her in Lapland when he didn't have to.

At the meeting he'd deferred to her. Made her feel seen. Even her life choices—that her mother was critical of— had been simply accepted by Lukas because she'd made them. *He* wasn't critical, because he trusted her to make the right choices for herself.

And now that *she* was the one struggling with the media attention, Lukas hadn't been smug. He didn't ask her how she liked it or say 'I told you so,' he'd opened up to her and helped her through it.

That man didn't deserve to be alone. Especially not at Christmas. Which had given her a brilliant idea. She had slipped from the uber-luxurious apartment and returned with all manner of decorations.

Green fir garlands now hung around the room. Woven through the gold poles with warm white fairy lights twinkling prettily between red and gold ornaments. The tree, which perfectly matched the garlands, was almost done. Katherine had only a few decorations left to hang. She quickly did so, then got rid of all the packaging before Lukas could see. There was one last thing to do, which she hoped he would do with her. Place the angel at the very top.

She'd just placed a plate on the coffee table when a gruff voice right behind her said, 'What's this?'

Katherine spun around, heart racing. 'I didn't hear you.'

Lukas placed his fingers on the pulse point on her neck, which did nothing to slow the beats down.

'You didn't answer my question,' he said softly.

Katherine was hit by a wave of doubt. Had she overstepped?

'I wanted to show you that you can celebrate the holidays,' she said. 'That you aren't alone.'

'Is that true?'

They stood exactly as they were. His hand on her neck. Her hands at her sides. Not moving a muscle. Not daring to breathe.

'Yes.'

For as long as he allowed her to be part of his world, he wouldn't be alone. So she stepped closer to him and wrapped her arms around his neck, not trying to kiss him or push for that passion that they so often lost themselves in, but just wanting to hold him. Give him the comfort he had been giving her.

His arms closed around her and he dropped his head onto her shoulder. In that moment Katherine could have wept. She had never felt his heart so open to her. A sign that this wasn't just physical.

'Is that lebkuchen?' he asked before she could overthink what was happening.

'Yes.' They broke apart as he instantly reached for one. 'Abandoned for biscuits,' she tsked.

But Lukas had halted. Held the confectionary in his hand, making no move to eat it.

'Lukas, it's the off-season and it's nearly Christmas. I think you can allow yourself a few things that make you happy.'

He turned a burning gaze to her. She knew only part of that intensity was because of the lebkuchen and the nostalgia he would certainly be feeling.

Shaking himself out of whatever it was that had a hold on him, Lukas brought the biscuit up to her lips.

'After my mother left, at Christmas my father would make sure we never ran out of these,' he said. She bit into the soft, spicey glory, listening almost as if hypnotised. 'Most years there weren't any presents, but there was always a tin of these for me to open on Christmas Eve.'

He popped the other half into his mouth. She was mesmerised by his lips.

Katherine remembered Lukas saying his father had been a cook. 'Did he bake them?'

He nodded.

'How long has it been since you had any?'

'Nearly two years.'

Because his father had died the year before. They couldn't have spent last Christmas together. He had no one to spend it with anymore. A holiday filled with pain. Well, she was about to change that.

'I have one more thing to do on the tree. Will you help me with it?'

'Of course.'

She tugged him by the hand and gave him a box to open but he was inspecting a gold nut on the tree. There were many scattered among the branches.

'You thought of everything.'

'Never underestimate a determined woman, Mr Jäger.'

'I would never underestimate you.'

'Open that.' She tried to hide her flushed cheeks but it was no use. He caught her chin and placed a soft kiss on her lips. The first kiss since the restaurant.

He let her go and opened the box, revealing an exquisite iridescent shell angel with gold metalwork.

'Will you put it up top?' she asked.

'As you wish.'

While he worked to get it out of the box, she told him of a memory. 'When we were younger, the four of us would decorate the tree under my parents' supervision but there was always a fight for who got to place the tree topper.'

Lukas stopped what he was doing to listen to her.

'At first we had an angel. It was porcelain and so beautiful. We promised to be careful but when the others fought, it broke. From then on we had a plastic star. Whenever the fight broke out, I'd slink away to the corner, as far as possible from the fray.'

'What did you do for attention?' Lukas asked.

'What do you mean?' she asked, bundling up the fallen tissue paper, but he pulled it from her hands and brought her closer to him.

'It's clear to me to that you didn't get much attention and your siblings' behaviour would have attracted a lot of it. But you still wanted it, didn't you? Even though you sat there in the corner away from them, watching. So what did you do to earn it from your parents?'

Katherine stood there dumbstruck. A mouth full of cotton. She couldn't answer his question, which made her throat burn with emotions she didn't want to express.

'I think you chose this job to be seen, Katherine,' he said so simply, as if he wasn't about to strip away her armour, leaving her vulnerable.

'You and your father shared a love of Alpha One and maybe becoming a driver wasn't an option but given what you've told me, you could have chosen other routes. Engineering, perhaps. But you chose journalism. A job that would have you seen and heard by millions.' He caressed her cheek. 'Attention.'

She tried to look away but he wouldn't let her.

'You spent so long trying to be the good daughter who didn't need anything that you made yourself nearly invisible. You did what was asked of you when it was asked with no pushback ever, but you wanted to be noticed by your parents and the only time you were was when it came to racing and this career path. And you want to take care of them because you are good and kind but also so that they'll finally take notice of you. So now, here you are in the public eye demanding attention, standing your ground in your life because you have always been independent. But from your mother's point of view…she doesn't understand why you've changed. Why you suddenly won't listen to her advice and won't be invisible anymore.'

Katherine could feel her throat burning but she didn't want to cry. Not in front of anyone. Not even Lukas.

'You wanted to be so good, so easy to deal with that you hid yourself from them, but they should have worked harder to know you.' His warm hand cupped the back of hers, turning it over and in it, he placed the angel. 'I see you, Katherine.'

Then he picked her up and took her to the tree where she easily placed the tree topper.

Her heart was going to burst. She wanted to cling onto Lukas and never let go.

'We still have to make an appearance,' he started when he set her down.

In an instant she went from floating to falling. This was still a fake relationship. He had been given no way to refuse. She could never forget that.

'Tomorrow, I will take us out on my boat,' Lukas went on. 'We'll be seen quite easily but we'll be alone.' She shivered as he tucked a lock of red hair behind her ear. 'The paps can get their pictures, but we'll have complete privacy.'

'Tomorrow is your thirty-fourth birthday,' she said, feeling foolish for having bought him a gift.

'You knew that?'

'The world knows that, Lukas,' she deadpanned.

'I meant, you remembered.'

'Of course, I did.'

'Why? And don't tell me for your work.'

Well, there went that excuse. The truth was she didn't know. Most drivers celebrated their birthday during the season but not Lukas, so the date should have meant nothing to her. And yet she was always aware of it.

'I can't answer that.'

'Can't or won't?' he pushed.

'I don't know why.'

'I think you do but you don't want to think about the reason. It's okay, Katherine, I understand.'

He had it wrong. There was nothing to think about.

'I need to shower,' he said.

He didn't ask for her to join him, neither did she follow him when he left the room. She was left in the beautifully decorated lounge, alone, confused, heart racing for no explicable reason.

CHAPTER FOURTEEN

WHEN LUKAS HAD said 'boat' Katherine hadn't been sure what to expect. Yes, she had seen pictures of him on board—taken by paparazzi with their telephoto lenses—but the truth was that while she loved fast cars, she knew virtually nothing about boats. This one was bigger than her apartment, and far more luxurious too. But it wasn't anywhere near as fast as she had expected it to be. Lukas threw himself out of planes, raced cars, went skiing and mountain biking; she expected that to translate to the water.

'You seem surprised.' He looked amused.

'It's slower than I thought it would be,' she confessed, hugging her arms in her thick cable-knit sweater. Lukas stood at a large silver wheel, steering the boat easily, with Katherine at his side. They were going out just far enough to be alone, which was why they were up on the fly bridge and not inside at the main helm.

'I come out here to get away from everything. I don't need it to be fast, I need it to be calming.' Lukas stopped the boat, mooring them at a point out on the water from which Katherine could see all of Monaco. It was a completely different place during race weekends. Now it looked spectacularly beautiful, calm, peaceful. Though it would never again be peaceful for her.

Now every future trip would be full of memories of Lukas.

His arms snaked around her waist.

Just an appearance, Katherine. This was his idea.

'Let's go down to the rear deck.'

His lips trailed up her neck causing a rush of excitement within her but her body reacting so readily to him also saddened her.

Are you wanting more from Lukas?

Before, she would have said 'no,' a flat out honest refusal. But she didn't know anymore.

He led her down to the rear of the boat furnished with plush couches around a fixed table.

'Have a seat, I'll be right back.'

From the couch she kept her eye on the principality, guessing from this distance where his apartment would be. Maybe she was growing too attached. Maybe she should leave. Lukas knew what her deal was. She couldn't change her mind on relationships, so he would understand if she made an excuse to go back to London.

After promising to stay for Christmas?

She didn't want to hurt him and pulled out a small gift box from her handbag.

'What's that?' Lukas asked, placing a plate of fruit on the table.

He sat close to her and her hand automatically went to his thigh as if she couldn't stand to not touch him. His hand closed around hers, keeping it there. Beneath the table where no one could see. No photographer would spy such a small, private show of affection. And it confused her more.

She placed the box in front of Lukas. 'Your birthday present.'

With his free hand, he pulled away at the ribbons and

opened the box. She watched him pull out a crystal snow-flake ornament.

'Seemed appropriate.'

He grinned. 'I'd say so.' With the ribbon the snowflake was attached to threaded around his middle finger, Lukas picked up the plate and stood. The sea breeze ruffled his light brown hair and plastered his sweater to his torso. 'Come with me.'

Lukas turned to walk through the glass doors, wait-ing for her just inside and shut them as soon as she was through.

'I thought we had to make a public appearance. What are we doing?'

'This is just for us, Katherine.' He took her hand and she paid no attention to the luxurious living area or the rooms they passed on the way to the main cabin, which was decorated in dark woods and soft lighting.

'Don't get stuck in your head,' Lukas said. 'This doesn't have to mean more than you want it to, but we've met our obligation, and I really don't want to share this part of you with anyone.' He sat Katherine on the edge of the bed, placing the plate down beside her and the snowflake next to it. 'Have I read your gift wrong? This is a reminder that we're temporary, is it not? Is no strings sex like we had in the cabin not what you want?'

Katherine had bought him that snowflake because no matter what happened between them, they would always have Lapland, the place where they connected with each other, memories of how good they could be together. But she could see how he would interpret it as a symbol of what they'd shared there, passion with an expiry date, and only that. A reminder that they were always meant to be temporary. She could have corrected his understanding, but what difference would it make? This wasn't forever.

'I want you, Lukas.' That was an irrefutable truth and the best deflection she could think of.

Lukas knelt before her, taking off her shoes one by one. 'Silly Katherine,' he said, moving to pop the button on her jeans, then pulling off her sweater. 'You can't want what you already have.'

But she didn't have him, not really.

I can pretend I do.

As soon as Lukas had said the words, he wanted to take them back because now Katherine would overthink them. She was falling for him, he saw it in the things she did, the words she said, in her eyes that hid so little, but she didn't *want* to. She was with him to save her career. If she was starting to feel more, she would likely quash those feelings because her success would always come first. He understood that. Respected it, even, because that was how he'd ended up in this situation too.

Except he couldn't lie to himself. What he felt for Katherine was far more than just passion or lust. The problem was they could never be more because she was still a journalist, and he didn't want a life lived in the media.

You've found a way around that right now.

A few weeks wasn't a lifetime.

A lifetime wasn't what Katherine wanted.

So now it was up to him to help them focus on something else. Get them out of their heads.

He lay Katherine on the bed and peeled off the rest of her clothes, dropping them to the floor and leaving her wearing nothing but the gold ring on her finger. Then he took off his own clothing, smirking as the look in her eyes changed from pensive to hungry.

He crawled over her, letting his skin brush hers, but he didn't kiss her in any bruising, intoxicating way. He kissed her lightly. Teasingly. Maddeningly. And when she tried to push up on her elbows to reach his lips, he grabbed her wrists and pinned them above her head.

'You don't get to rush this.' He wanted to take his time because when it came to Katherine, time was very much a finite resource. One day soon she would be gone and this connection that was more powerful than anything he'd shared with anyone else would be gone too.

'You're a damn tease, Lukas,' she complained.

'I am.' He reached over to the plate and plucked a piece of mango. 'But I'm a nice tease. I see that hungry look—' he leaned down to whisper in her ear '—and I'll feed it.' His cock twitched and at the same time, he brought the piece of fruit to her mouth and she obediently bit into it with a moan. Juice glossed her lips and ran down his fingers. He put the rest of the piece in his own mouth, savouring the sweetness. Katherine freed a hand and pulled his towards her, licking the tracks of juice up his skin to his fingers, which she took into her mouth, sucking them clean one digit at a time. It was his turn to moan out loud.

'And I'll happily take it all,' she husked.

Damn this woman. 'You're killing all the restraint I have.'

'Then let go.'

'I want to make this special for you,' Lukas confessed.

'Why?'

'Because I'm certain you've misunderstood my intentions for bringing you here today. You got so quiet after I told you what we'd be doing today—that we'd be making an appearance. I didn't say it to remind you of the state of things between us. I said it so you'd know that I respect your commitment to your career, that I wouldn't jeopardise it, which means showing up publicly. But I also wanted you to myself, Katherine.' He ran his nose up her neck, inhaling her scent. A scent that he both craved and didn't want in his bedroom because when she left and it lingered, it would be torment. 'And right now, we're perfectly alone. No one can see us. No one can hear us. You're mine and I'm yours.'

Katherine closed the gap between them, kissing him savagely and he wished that it wasn't just for right now. He wished things could be different. He wished he could call himself Katherine's without any quantifiers. But that wasn't reality. Reality was the ache in the base of his abdomen from how badly he craved her. It was his brain clouding over from the touch of her tongue to his. It was the pleasure encompassing his whole body as if he'd dived head first into a pool of pure ecstasy.

He needed her to know this pleasure too.

So he broke away from her lips, his stomach somersaulting from the half-blind way she looked at him—lust in her dilated pupils—and he kissed a path down her chest. He stopped to worship at her breasts, his body moving with hers as she writhed.

'Lukas,' she whimpered, 'more.'

He grazed her nipple, revelling in the way she cried out and continued kissing down her body until he was hovering above her sex. Her skin glistened with her arousal, making him curse under his breath. There was a look of anticipation in her eyes that matched the feeling burning through his body. He needed her. Wanted her. And he would have her now over and over so that she would chant his name until it was so embedded in her soul, she would never be free of him because he would never be free of her either.

His mouth closed over her smooth skin, his tongue delving through her folds as he sucked her clit into his mouth making her shout his name. He'd never known such satisfaction. He was thankful they were on the boat so no one would hear them but wished with equal measure that they were somewhere public so everyone would know it was his name on her lips. And maybe in her heart.

He feasted on Katherine, drinking from her as her breaths grew louder and her moans more insistent. Until she was pulling on her hair and on his. Until she was fisting the covers and bucking her hips. Locking her legs around his shoulders, he reached towards her with his hands so she could grab on to them. A tether as she threw her head back and screamed out her release.

Her hands grew slack and then she was running her fingers through her fiery red hair, eyes still scrunched shut and Lucas needed her in his arms through her journey back to earth. So he lay on his side beside her and pulled her to his chest, but it wasn't enough. He needed to be closer. He grabbed her thigh, hooking it over his naked hip, sliding his hard aching cock into her slick heat, groaning animalistically as he watched her face. His heart racing. Consumed by her taste, and her smell and her satin skin.

'Yes,' she said in a laboured breath with a content smile and flushed cheeks.

How was he ever going to say goodbye?

He had been protecting himself by keeping her in her own room, but tonight that would change. From this point on she would sleep in his bed and leave her presence all over his home. He would enjoy every bit of having Katherine tied to him while he could.

Until Lukas thrust into Katherine, making her sing a litany of moans and whimpers, he hadn't known a heart could soar and hurt at the same time. But Katherine's hands caressed his cheek, and he didn't care.

'More,' he begged. 'Touch me everywhere.'

Mark me for life.

'You're ruining me,' she said so close to his lips that they were breathing in each other's pants.

'You already have.' He tried to memorise her roving touch on his chest and back and hair. His hands travelled the length of her body, followed the perfect curve of her ass. Fingers digging into the soft flesh, and Katherine's movements, matching his, became more urgent. Any hope he had that he could take his time went out the window as he started thrusting harder, faster. Lost to sensation and lust and everything Katherine made him feel.

There was a coiling in his spine. Every nerve ending screaming for release.

'I—I'm so close,' Katherine stuttered through a frantic breath.

'Touch yourself.' He wanted her feeling as much pleasure as it was humanly possible to experience. He took her hand from his hair, brought it to his mouth, licking her middle finger and slid it between their bodies, making her gasp but he could feel her climax building in her body. In the way she gripped around him.

'Come for me, Katherine,' Lukas ordered. Demanded. Begged.

And then she was clutching onto him in a violent hold, her voice going hoarse as wave after wave of her climax washed over her pulling Lukas into the most intense release of his life.

'Fuck,' he growled, holding tightly on to her. He couldn't

let go. He couldn't open his eyes. But he felt wetness fall from Katherine's face onto his arm and he knew exactly what she felt. This was different. This was so much more than any other time they had sex because this wasn't sex.

This time, out on the water, they made love.

They made love.

He loved her.

A woman he could never have. A woman fighting for her career in the media. The very same media he hated, but she was different. She had integrity, she was selfless and kind. And he trusted her.

He trusted her enough to be physical with her when he hadn't been with anyone for three years. He trusted her enough to confide in her about his mother…his career.

What would it be like to be with her?

Their whole relationship would be in the public eye. People would think he was accepting of the media because he was with one of them. But right now they were in his boat because he had found a way around the attention.

Could he do this all the time? Did he want to live his life this way for the woman he loved?

CHAPTER FIFTEEN

KATHERINE WATCHED LUKAS with a smile as he set a little Christmas tree on the table that sat between two armchairs in perfect view from his bed.

It was the first time she had set foot in here and it felt like they had moved beyond their agreement of just pleasure. Something had changed on the boat. Well, something had been changing before that but when she and Lukas had slept together earlier, it had been better than anything that had come before. There had been all the passion and fun she had come to expect but there had also been an intensity. A connection so strong between them she'd wanted to cling onto Lukas and never let go.

She didn't even know why she had cried but her heart had been about to burst.

Now she was in his bedroom. Proof that Lukas, that viciously private man, had lowered his walls for her.

'You know, you have a pretty large one of those two floors below you,' she said, gesturing at the small tree.

'But that tree won't have this.' He pulled out the snowflake she had given him and hung it on a branch. 'This is just for me.'

Lukas would never change. Hardly anyone came into his home and still he wanted to put barriers around what they shared. Hoard as much of the relationship for himself so no one else could peer in. Did he realise that that kind of behaviour made people more curious?

'Come here,' he called as he kicked off his shoes and settled on the large bed with one arm under his head, the other stretched out beckoning her.

She couldn't resist.

She joined him, marvelling at how tranquil, how content she was when his arm curled around her.

'I suppose that's a pretty good spot for it,' she said. 'In the morning, when the sun catches the crystal—'

'You'll be here to see it because you'll be in my bed.' He hovered over her and she ran her fingers over his soft lips.

'I thought you wanted some separation.' An assumption based on him having given her a room on a different floor. Her workspace was also away from his. So this was a big change. One that emphasized how real the feelings in this fake romance were becoming.

'I want you in my arms and in my home, Katherine. We might not be blessed with a lot of time, but we can make the most of what we've been given.'

But what if they had more time? She could wake up beside Lukas on some mornings, on others she would wake to the scent of coffee and him shirtless and sweaty. She could work in the office he provided her. Maybe they would travel to the tracks together. He'd race and she would report and then they would come back to each other every night. That didn't seem so bad. He'd had a vasectomy so there was no risk of a family that might force her to give up her dreams.

With Lukas, she was safe to pursue the life she wanted.

'I want that too,' she whispered, and he kissed her. It

was volcanic. Their passion erupting around them. Sweeping them away and then a loud ping pierced the air.

Katherine groaned. 'I need to check that. It could be work.' It most likely was.

Lukas loosened his hold, and she pulled her phone out of her pocket and saw a new email from Jennifer. She opened the email and her stomach sank.

...I know you asked me not to run the article... Katherine read ...but it will be out tomorrow.

Tomorrow!

No. No! This couldn't be happening!

'What's wrong?' Lukas asked.

'I'm not sure yet. I need to call Jennifer.' She tried to hide her trembling and gave Lukas a crushing kiss. This call would be make-or-break for them.

Katherine went down to the lounge, as far away from Lukas as she could get, and called her editor. Jennifer answered immediately.

'You said you'd pull the article.' Katherine didn't bother with pleasantries now. This was a disaster. Lukas could never see what she had written. Those words felt like a lifetime ago.

'I know I did, but there's so much buzz around you two right now, Kat. That article is a goldmine.'

Katherine pulled off the ring she wore on her free hand, anxiously toying with it while she tried to figure out a way to get Jennifer to change her mind.

'That's not the truth. Tell me why you're really publishing it,' she demanded.

'You want the truth? Fine. The truth is we asked the two of you to pose as a couple. Generate interest. What we got is a shopping expedition, Lukas trying to hide you away from the cameras and some shots of you standing on a boat.'

Every one of those moments was so much more than Jennifer made them sound. Right now, Katherine was in a room filled with Christmas decorations because that was how far they had come. 'That's enough to hint at a relationship, Jennifer.'

'Did we ask for hints? We wanted you to leave the meeting hand in hand. What does that tell you, Kat? I warned you in that meeting what would happen.'

'Warned me? Bringing up the article was more like blackmail, Jennifer. We established that the things I wrote aren't true. We have more information now that surely warrants a rewrite.' Maybe if she could speak to Lukas, she could pen something that he would be happy with being out in the world. A piece that didn't shatter this dream they had only just found.

'They aren't untrue, Kat. There's still a valid angle here,' Jennifer said, 'And having the article come from you is going to blow up traffic to the site, which is what I care about. But you know the others will be happy too, because people will tune in just to see what happens between you and Lukas in the aftermath.'

She was nauseous.

'Is there any way at all I can convince you not to run it. Anything?' She knew she sounded desperate now but she didn't care. The thoughtful man up in his room who had made her feel seen and protected deserved better.

She deserved better.

'No.'

'Damn it, Jennifer!'

Katherine hung up. She couldn't speak. She sank into the couch cushions and covered her face with her trembling hands. Lukas was going to hate her. All this contentment they'd found would be lost.

She had to find a way to get out ahead of it and the only way to do that was to talk to Lukas. After all, he knew what their dynamic was like. He knew she didn't hate him anymore. If she could get him to see reason, maybe it wouldn't be so bad.

She had to try. She couldn't lose him.

Lukas stood out on the balcony attached to his bedroom, leaning on the glass balustrade, watching the sun sink lower towards the sparkling horizon. Katherine had been gone awhile, but he understood how important her career was to her. Just how much her need to be successful stemmed from a need to be seen by her family. And while he was still struggling with the fact that her career required so much publicity, that it was in itself so invasive, he also wanted to be with her. For now, she was in his bed.

Even once she left and all the Christmas decorations were packed away, he would still leave that snowflake out. It was the only way he would never lose her, because he would never lose the memory.

One way or another he was determined that he would start the new season in the paddock. And Katherine would undoubtedly be there. How would it feel to see her? How would it feel when he got out of the car with adrenaline still pumping and emotions running high, then had to be interviewed by her?

You don't know that you'll be in a car.

He still had to face the fact that he was currently without a drive, but they were all working towards that goal.

You still haven't turned down the team principal offer.

He hadn't and he wasn't sure why, when he belonged behind the wheel. It was what he'd always wanted. What his father had wanted. Being a racer made him worth something. But Katherine had also made some valid points when he told her about Vortex's offer. Points that he had been thinking about.

'Lukas?'

He turned around to find Katherine standing in the middle of his bedroom, clutching her phone in both hands. There was something about the way she awkwardly shifted her weight from foot to foot. The way she looked off to the side as if she was avoiding his gaze.

He immediately went on high alert. Something was wrong.

'What's happened?' he asked. She opened and closed her mouth but no sound escaped. 'Come here, Katherine.' He held his hand out to her and to his relief she walked towards him. When she was close enough, he put an arm around her waist, the other caressing her cheek as he placed a small kiss on her forehead.

'Whatever is wrong, we can fix it.' He would do nearly anything for her.

'Something has happened.' She swallowed hard. He could tell she was trying not to let her eyes well up. He never wanted to see her cry.

'Take your time.'

'Please hear me out before you say or do anything. Can you promise me? Please?'

'Of course.'

She nodded, pressed her lips together then said, 'Before we went to Lapland, before I even knew about Lapland actually, I had to write a feature on you for Aero's site.'

The words had irritation flooding through his system because anything involving media attention was never good for him. And if Katherine had written something before, they were trapped together, it was definitely going to be bad. But he couldn't respond as he usually did because it was his Katherine standing before him. Not the woman he'd hated, who'd hated him in return. So, fighting as hard as he could, he suppressed his irritation enough to respond calmly. 'And it's coming out now.'

He didn't like the idea, but if he had given it any thought he would have realised that she must have tons of work submitted that would only be published now. The truth was that he hadn't thought about it, because he was so lost in her. Another tendril of annoyance rose to the surface as he realised that fact, but he pushed it back too.

Stay calm. You don't know what she's going to say. It could be easily fixed.

'We've moved past the hate, Katherine, and if it's anything like what you've written before I've already seen it all.'

But she shook her head. 'No, you haven't,' she said gruffly. 'I called Jennifer after the helicopter ride and asked her to kill this article. She said she would.'

'But she hasn't.'

'No, she hasn't.'

'How bad is it?' Katherine wouldn't answer. 'Katherine, I asked you a question.' Still there was no response. And suddenly the sun lost all warmth. He was cold. Standing on a precipice. But it didn't have to be that way. Maybe if he could see what she'd said, they could figure out a way forward.

'Show it to me.'

Katherine stepped away from him, a pleading look in her eyes. 'Can we talk about this first? Do you really want to see it? We've come so far from the people we were.'

'We are still those people, we've just learned to understand each other. But I have to tell you that I don't like
the fact that you don't want me to see it. When is it coming out?'

'Tomorrow,' she whispered.

'Great, then Dominic should know all about it.' Lukas
turned to walk back into the bedroom, ready to call his
manager.

'No. Wait!'

'One way or another, I will see it.'

'I know.' She covered her face. 'I just don't want you
to yet.'

'There's no point in putting it off.'

Katherine tapped the screen of her phone a few times
and then handed the device to him before taking several
steps back until she was against the balustrade. As if she
had to get a safe distance away from him.

'I feel sick,' she said more to herself than him but he
could see it in her face, and it was this reaction that made
him so adamant that he know what she had written. He
looked down at the screen in his hand and began reading.

*Lukas Jäger: One of the Greats or Overrated Has-
Been?*

*A truth of Alpha One is that you're only as good as
your last race. For Lukas Jäger, it has been a season to
forget. Outside of showing brief glimpses of a talent he
once possessed, it has otherwise been twenty-three races
of mistakes, spins and slow practice times, which begs the
question: Are we really surprised that he was replaced by
Easton Rivers? The answer is no.*

Lukas looked at Katherine, who had hugged herself,
standing silently awaiting her judgement. She'd been there
at those races. She knew the spins had been caused by a

bad aerodynamics package. The practice times had been slow until they found a workable set-up for the race. Lukas had outqualified Will, his teammate, twenty races to three and finished all but one race ahead of him, and that one slip-up had been due to mechanical issues.

He went back to reading without saying a word.

But before we analyse his past season, perhaps we should look at his rise through the ranks thanks to experienced race manager, Dominic Wilson. Coming from a part of Austria not renowned for producing any racer of significance, Lukas received a lot of attention from the start...

Lukas could feel his pulse racing faster after each word.

...an argument could be made that, in his winning years, a lack of serious competition likely made him appear far more skilled a driver than he was. He did in fact have the most dominant car on the grid, which often meant he had no one to race, due to him starting from pole position.

With each excerpt that stood out to him, the calm he promised slipped away and was replaced with fury. This article covered his life in the worst way.

The question on people's lips right now is: Were Florian Jäger's sacrifices worth it? A year or two ago, even in seasons that weren't Jäger's best, perhaps an argument could be made that they had been. But after this year, one could no longer answer that question with a definitive yes.

This was Katherine's magnum opus. Her masterpiece of all the pieces of utter hate she had written. She now knew exactly how badly Lukas needed to honour his father's memory, and perhaps she had seen it before. After all, they seemed to understand each other in the strangest way, so she'd known what a nerve writing this would strike.

Often described as cold by members of the paddock,

Lukas has earned a reputation for being ruthless and self-ish. He would be seen walking around with a notebook for the weekend. Data on the car, tyre performance and conditions collected from his observations, which he steadfastly refused to share with his teammates on the other side of the garage. Noted commentator Benjamin Stevens called the move immature and unfair. After all, it was the team that had to win the constructors' championship to remain competitive and to reward all the men and women working hard at the factory.

But no feature would be complete without a look at off-track antics as well. Jäger's publicist, Erin Walker, had her hands full after the scandal surrounding the strained relationship between him and his mother came to light—when it became clear that she had been all but exiled from their small Austrian hometown, where her son is hero-worshipped. In a sport like Alpha One where the media is your friend, Jäger opted to shun all attempts to get his side of the story, leading many to speculate about his culpability in her fate.

Lukas sat in the chair beside the small Christmas tree with the twinkling snowflake and read to the end.

...so we would have to say signing William Bell and Easton Rivers was a genius decision from Thomas Dudek, who has now secured a young, scandal-free, talented duo that will take the team back to the top. As for Lukas Jäger, it was a good career while it lasted but perhaps bowing out of the sport now would be his wisest move. There's no denying his wealth of knowledge; perhaps a consultant role at a smaller team should be his next career choice.

Clack.

In the silent room the sound of Lukas placing the phone on the table beside him was as loud as a shout.

'Lukas, say something,' Katherine begged from the balcony.

He pressed his fingers to his forehead. 'What would you like me to say?' His voice was empty.

A sharp pain cut through his chest, his heart aching, his pulse thrumming. These words had eviscerated him. This article was going to undo all the work he, Dominic and Erin had done to win him a seat. The woman he loved would be the reason his career ended, and he could feel from the tone of the writing that that was exactly what she had wanted.

'Was this revenge for me accidentally getting you fired?'

'What? No? I'd like to think I'm more professional than that,' Katherine said defensively. 'I—I didn't know you like I do now. I told Jennifer we couldn't run it because it wasn't the truth anymore.'

Lukas laughed at that. Heat radiated from his eyes. His teeth ground together but he laughed. 'It was never the truth.'

He looked at her and she shrunk away from whatever she saw on his face, but then he witnessed her screw up her courage and approach him.

'Please, Lukas, please understand things were different when I wrote that.' She knelt at his feet and took his hands in hers. All he wanted to do was shove her away but he couldn't because even though he was furious and hurt, he always, *always* wanted more of her. It was infuriating. 'It was before you showed me who you are. Jennifer blackmailed me with this article in that meeting at Aero. If I didn't agree to fake a relationship with you, she was going to release the article. I couldn't let that happen. I told her I'd write something else. I thought you could have a say in it. I tried to fix this before it got out. I tried to make sure you weren't hurt.'

And then Lukas did push her away. He got to his feet, marching angrily away from her. Looking around wildly for some way to calm down but there was no use because Katherine was lying.

'That's bullshit and you know it,' he spat. 'You had several opportunities to come clean with this. In Lapland when you knew it would run, you had your phone and your laptop but stayed quiet. All the time here, even though you asked for the article to be killed you could have confessed and been open with me. You hid it and still you've made no apology.'

'Lukas, I'm—'

'Don't fucking say it now, Katherine. Just don't.' He gripped his hair tightly in his hands, the pain a welcome distraction. He felt stupid for ever trusting her. For falling so hard for her. 'The woman who wrote this would have no problem coming into my life under false pretences. I think this person—' he said, pointing at the phone '—would have cooked up a scheme with Robert and Courteney just to get those extra clicks.'

'That's not true.' She tried to cross the room to him but he wanted none of it.

'I should have seen it from the start. You only got close to me for a story.'

Katherine didn't stop the tears then. 'I would never do that!'

Lukas had enough. He went to Katherine and wiped the tears from her eyes. For all he knew, she was faking them. 'And to think that it was my good word that got you this job at Aero.' Her eyes widened, jaw slackened at his words, and he took pleasure in her shock. 'I told them it wouldn't hurt to have a beautiful woman who knows the sport on the presenter team. I said the drivers wouldn't mind talking to you.'

'You hated me.'

Lukas dropped his hand to his side. 'Leave.'

'You hated me!' Katherine cried, near hysterical.

'I didn't at first,' he said softly. A finality to his tone as he took a step back. 'Leave.'

'I don't want to,' Katherine said, her voice broken. 'Christmas is days away, I don't want to leave you.'

'Get out, Katherine.'

'Lukas, please. Maybe take some time to calm down and then we can talk.'

'I said get out!' he yelled. They stood there, staring at each other until she dropped her gaze and walked out of his bedroom.

He wanted no one in his home. Least of all this person who could be so utterly hateful towards him, even while he loved her. Never again. He was done with the media and done with love.

CHAPTER SIXTEEN

KATHERINE PULLED UP to a cream, three-bedroom semi-detached house in St Albans. A house she visited as frequently as was possible. A house that she'd grown up in, dreaming about a big career in London. She had no idea if her parents were home but as soon as she got off the plane from Nice—having spent the night at the airport waiting for the first flight out that morning—barely able to keep herself together, this was the only place she wanted to go.

She couldn't get Lukas's revelation out of her head. She blamed him all this time for almost destroying her career and maybe he did, but he was also the reason she was successful now. That she had a better role at Aero than at VelociTV. And she had used that opportunity only afforded to her because of Lukas to try to convince the world to hate him. To see the worst in him.

Her eyes misted up again, so she switched off her Mercedes and walked up to the door. Unable to hear any voices inside, she pulled out her spare key and let herself in.

'Mum? Dad?' she called, but there was no immediate answer. All the willpower she had to not fall apart ebbed away. The dam walls were fracturing and out spouted jets of anguish. She could feel her face crumble but she tried so hard to breathe through the pain of losing Lukas. A man she would have had to say goodbye to anyway but when he was kicking her out, she'd realised she didn't want to leave. She never wanted to say goodbye to him.

She turned to leave. 'This was a mistake.'

'Kittykat? I thought I heard your voice.'

Before she'd realised what she was doing, she spun around and launched herself at her father, who caught her in a tight hug. She never got so emotional that her parents had to comfort her. She could modulate her emotions on her own. Had done so since she was young.

No one else did.

No, her siblings didn't. They expected comfort.

She pulled away from her father, looking at the textured cream tiles that hadn't changed in twenty-seven years.

'This is unlike you,' her father said, his hand on her shoulder.

But was it? She did get upset. She'd been upset when her father had missed important days in her life because of Paige. She'd just made sure to mask it so that he wouldn't feel guilty.

...they should have worked harder to know you.

That thought of Lukas made it impossible to speak.

'Come, let's have some tea and we can chat in the living room. I have a fire going.'

'Can I have a coffee instead?' It wouldn't be like Lukas's, but she loved coffee and she missed him.

'Since when do you like coffee?' her dad asked as he reached into the back of the cupboard to pull out a jar of instant.

'I always have.' Katherine wasn't sure what made her say it. She was here to seek comfort, not to make her parents feel guilty.

He hummed as he switched on the kettle. 'I'm the only

one here. Your mother is out with Paige, and your brothers are off somewhere.'

'That's fine.' She really only wanted her dad.

He finished making the drinks and handed a floral mug to Katherine. She took a sip of the milky coffee. It wasn't great but at least it was something she had asked for.

'Let's go talk.'

The lounge had remained unchanged. The walls were still a shade of peach she could almost taste. The comfortable, pillowy couches were in exactly the same places even if the upholstery had been replaced a few times over the years, always with exactly the same colour and fabric. In the corner stood a Christmas tree with a plastic angel on top. A new plastic angel.

'Who put the angel up?' Katherine asked, sitting in the chair farthest from the tree while her father sat next to it.

'Christopher won this round, though there were casualties.'

'I see that.'

'So tell me what's wrong, Kittykat. I imagine it has something to do with Lukas Jäger.'

It was a physical ache to hear his name.

'Do you want to explain what happened? One moment you were coming to dinner, the next you were missing and then you're in a relationship with a man I know you dislike. I've never had to worry about you, Kat, but these past few weeks have been worrying.'

Her father's words made her feel both angry and guilty. She never wanted them to worry about her and now she felt his disappointment in his words. Like she was being chastised.

'I know, Dad. I'm sorry. I found out about the Finland trip last minute and then Lukas and I got caught in the storm.' Katherine stopped. She didn't have to give her father the abridged version. He was her family. 'Actually, he saved me.'

'Saved you?'

And then Katherine told her father everything that had happened in Lapland, but she kept the passion a secret for herself. Even excluding that physical connection from the narrative, when Katherine looked back at their time, she realised how much they'd had together, how much more than lust. Even if they hadn't slept together, she would have left there wanting more of him. And then she confessed the truth about their relationship, how it had started. Saying it had all been fake felt like a lie.

Her father's eyes softened. He'd remained silent while she spoke, but now he moved across the room to sit beside Katherine, pulling her into a tight hug that made it hard to keep the tears at bay.

'It wasn't fake,' her father said softly, putting an arm around her shoulders and pulling out his phone from his pocket. Suddenly she was a young girl again watching racing with her father except this time she was the entertainment. He was showing her pictures of herself from news articles he had saved. And despite the devastation cracking her soul apart, a small piece of her shattered heart rejoiced because she was alone with her father getting a bit of the attention she had always craved.

'Look at this picture,' he said, swiping to one that was taken the day she and Lukas had gone shopping. 'Look at that smile on your face. Do you know when I last saw you smile like that?'

'No,' she breathed.

'Never,' he replied. 'And this one...' It was from the boat—Lukas holding a plate, her looking up at him. Was that only yesterday? 'Your mother hasn't ever looked at me like this and there hasn't been a day where the two of us have not been in love. Let me show you one more.' Her dad scrolled on his phone to a picture taken the night she and Lukas had gone to the casino. She was looking away but Lukas was looking at her. The emotion in his eyes took her breath away. 'That young man is not faking, and neither were you.'

'It didn't feel fake,' Katherine admitted, taking the phone from her father.

'What do you see? How does he look at you?' He squeezed her tighter.

'Like he'd fight the world for me. Like he'd hold back the oceans if I asked him to.' Except what they had wasn't meant to last. 'But he only agreed to this situation because he was forced to. He wants to drive. This PR stunt was his last shot at an offer.'

Her father took the phone from her and placed it on the scuffed coffee table then placed both arms around her. She wished she could have felt comfort like this growing up.

'How did he react in that meeting?'

'He asked for my opinion and then made sure I was okay.'

'I see, and after that?' her father pressed.

'He took me to his home that he allows very few into. He gave me privacy and comfort and support. He helped me when I was struggling…' with the media attention, with what her life was and why she chose this career. He never judged her. He kept her safe and treasured her and loved her.

And she loved him.

Katherine loved him so much it felt like a vital append-age had been lopped off. She loved him and she hadn't come clean to him about the article. Nor had she apologised.

'I never gave him the benefit of the doubt. After he cost me my job, I was convinced he was an awful person, but the truth was so very different.'

Was this revenge for me for accidentally getting you fired?

Maybe subconsciously, it all had been.

Katherine covered her mouth, muffling her voice. 'I was never impartial. If I had been I wouldn't have felt the need to pull that article in the first place.'

'Can you understand why he feels betrayed?' her father asked without judgement.

'It's my job,' she said but the words tasted wrong.

'I've always admired your commitment and your work ethic, but I have also always worried that you put achievement above everything else in your life. Sweetheart, it's not your job that makes you important or worth listening to. You already are. Allow yourself to be happy outside of your career.'

That brought Lukas's words straight back to mind.

You are not your mother. You have achieved so much more than everyone else in your family has. Why are you letting your mother's choices warn you away from a possible future?

That night she had felt so close to Lukas. And that kiss afterwards would never fade from memory. It broke her and mended her. Made her want to cry and levitate. It was so raw, so desperate. And the next morning had been even better. When he placed that angel in her hand it felt like a missing piece of her soul clicked into place.

She looked at the tired Christmas tree in the corner with its supermarket ornaments and brand new plastic angel.

A perfect reminder of the way she had been sidelined by her family.

'You say that yet you only had time for me when it came to racing or my career. Even then, when I finally broke into the industry you were gone to help Paige in another country.'

'Katherine—' Her father loosened his hold of her. Surprise on his face. But she spoke over him. She couldn't hold back the words this time.

'And how can I be happy and allow myself to love someone when Mum taught me that love means settling down and giving up my dreams? Dreams I worked bloody hard for. A career without which I wouldn't have even the little bit of attention you grant me now.' She got off the couch, tears she'd held back for years streaming down her face as she faced her father.

'Where is this coming from?' he asked. Hands on the couch, ready to stand, but Katherine ignored him. The dam had burst and nothing would stop the raging torrent.

'There's no winning, Dad. I either disappoint Mum, give up the connection I have with you, or forego love and companionship. I can't have it all. I never could!'

His eyes widened. 'Katherine, you know... I...' He paused, shaking his head. 'That's not true.'

'I love Christmas, did you know that?'

Again, her father shook his head. 'You always seemed above it. You never got as involved as your siblings.'

'Think, Dad! Think back to what it was actually like. I never saw the point of fighting with my siblings who didn't really want me in their club anyway. This year I got to put an angel on an amazing tree, and it was one of the best moments of my life. Lukas made me feel seen in a way no one else in my life ever has.' Her skin replayed the memory of him lifting her up so she could reach the top of the tree.

Her father looked as if he'd been struck.

'I've always liked coffee, Dad. Every time we went out it was the first thing I ordered and yet you still didn't know that I liked it.'

She could see the shame in her father's expression, and it hurt her to see it, but she wanted more from her family. Hell, she wanted more from the world. From her job. She wanted respect and recognition.

'I need to apologise to Lukas,' she said softly. 'And then I need to go to the office.'

'Do what you need to, Kittykat,' her father said gruffly, 'and maybe after that you and I can talk. Maybe I have some making up to do as well.'

'Dad,' she croaked, and he went to her, engulfing her in a hug.

When he pulled away, Katherine could see his lashes were wet. 'I'm proud of you and I love you and I've failed you, but I promise that will all change. Go make your call. I'll be right here waiting.'

Katherine raced up the stairs to the bedroom she used to share with Paige. She tried Lukas's number, praying he would answer, but it rang until she got his voicemail.

'Lukas, I know I messed up. I'm sorry. I'm sorry for the article, for how unfairly I treated you, for everything. Please, please can we talk?' She ended the call and sent a text. She held the phone in her hand, waiting. And waiting. And waiting. It had been delivered and seen but there was no response.

She had to find a way to get Lukas to talk to her. This man she loved didn't threaten her dream, he made her see a better one. And now she needed to fight for him.

CHAPTER SEVENTEEN

JENNIFER AND ROBERT were in the small meeting room when Katherine arrived at Aero TV. After a long talk with her father, she had called them requesting a meeting asap.

She was done being disrespected, had enough of her career being weaponised to control her. It ended now. Her heart pounded because she knew if this meeting went badly, it would be the end for her at the Alpha One official broadcaster. It would be a step backwards. The thought made her feel ill but enough was enough.

'What's this about, Kat?' Robert asked.

Katherine took her time pulling out a seat at the round table, ensuring she was visibly calm, then looked at him and Jennifer.

'We have some issues to discuss.' She placed her hands on the table. Fingers loosely knitted together.

'You're not still upset about the article, are you?' Jennifer asked. 'Do you want to see the traffic stats since it went live? It was great for you.'

'No, I don't.' Anger blazed through her. 'And it was great for you. Aero. Not me. Not Lukas.'

'What does Lukas Jäger matter? You were faking a relationship, badly I might add. Our needs are more important than any driver's.'

Katherine never wanted to work with Jennifer again. 'You have no respect for people's lives, Jennifer. No respect for my work or reputation. For that reason, I am quitting the column.'

Jennifer threw herself back in her chair with a huff. 'Don't be so dramatic, Kat.'

She battled for calm with all her might because she wanted to rage at these people. 'Let's look at the facts, shall we? With no concern for our well-being after being stuck in a snowstorm, Aero forced Lukas and me to pose as a couple purely for publicity. Threatened our careers, threatened my reputation by blackmailing me with the article that we both knew contained false information, but still you used it to control me.'

'*Control* is a bit harsh, don't you think?' Robert said.

'What would you call it?' She cast her glare on him. 'Either I was fired if I didn't comply or the article was released which would call into question my ethics and integrity, my ability to be impartial and truthful. It would paint me as ruthless to the point of unscrupulousness. Who would hire me after that? That *is* control, Robert.' She wanted to throw herself out of her chair and pace the room, but she couldn't be emotional here. 'Tell me, if I was a male journalist would either of you have demanded this of me? Toyed with my career like this? I suspect the answer is no.'

Robert looked away while Jennifer refused to say anything.

'So here's how things are going to go. First, you're going to pull the article and issue a retraction—'

'Absolutely not!' Jennifer all but yelled.

'I'm not done.' Katherine stared her down. 'Second, the manipulation of me and my career stops now. You told me about the trip to Lapland at the last possible moment, Robert, when you would have known long enough to acquire service providers to carve a literal track in the snow. I'm not a pawn to be used, I am a journalist and deserve to be treated with the same respect you give my male colleagues. Third, in the place of the column, I will be added to the panel on *Track Talk* every Tuesday night. I know this sport, have great insights and bloody good access to information.'

'Kat—' Robert tried but Katherine was on a roll.

'A producer who treated me abominably once told me to go complain on a talk show, and you know what? He was right. If you don't comply, I will tell the world what happened. How you must have been planning to capitalize off our experience in Lapland before you'd even checked that I was okay, how you forced Lukas and me into a public relationship for clicks.' Katherine could see Robert turning paler with every word. 'How I asked you, Jennifer, to kill the article and why and how you blackmailed me with it. How Scott Courteney threatened my job. You think Alpha One will want to remain bound to Aero TV after that? They'll find another network. And I will never stop talking about this. Never stop talking about the institutionalised misogyny. I refuse to be treated how you have treated me.'

Robert swallowed thickly. 'I'm sure we can come to an understanding.'

Katherine stood firm. 'I want your agreement and nothing less or I will walk out of here and into another network because you know I'm great at my job. My fan base will come with me. We all know that would be a substantial audience. How many people do you think will believe my story?'

'Fine,' he acceded. 'We have an agreement.'

CHAPTER EIGHTEEN

A VIBRATION ERUPTED from the nightstand beside Lukas.

He didn't react at all.

He didn't blink. Didn't move a muscle to answer the insistent phone. He just lay there in his bed. Staring. Katherine had been right. The morning sunshine streaming through the glass caught the crystal snowflake. Light refracted across his bedroom in slow walking prismatic rainbows. It was beautiful. He hated it.

Still, he looked at the snowflake.

His phone stopped ringing.

Katherine had been calling constantly. Had been texting and leaving voicemails begging him to talk to her but he had nothing to say. How did he put into words the swirling betrayal. How did he express to her that he trusted her even though he shouldn't have. That he had fallen in love with her.

His phone started ringing again.

Lukas tossed off the covers and got out of bed, noticing when he did that the name on the phone wasn't Katherine's, but Dominic's.

He snatched the phone up and answered quickly as he went down to his kitchen.

'Took you long enough to answer,' Dominic complained.

'Sorry, Dom, I thought you were—'

'Katherine.'

'Yes,' Lukas said. Mechanically, he put on a pot of coffee and walked the length of the floor as he waited. Moving from room to room.

'You saw the article,' Dominic said in a resigned tone.

'Yesterday. Why are you only calling me now? Shouldn't you have warned me about this?' Lukas's hard tone surprised himself. He wasn't angry at Dominic; he was angry at Katherine. Or was he? Lukas would have walked away from Katherine after Lapland if Dominic and Erin hadn't conspired with Aero to force him into dating her.

You didn't want to walk away though, did you?

'I thought it would be best to give you two time to work it out. I knew Katherine wouldn't blindside you.'

'You knew that, did you? Like you knew what she had written?' Lukas stepped into the decorated lounge. A smiling angel looking down at him. Laughing at his foolishness. Yesterday he'd wanted signs of Katherine all over his home. Today it was hell. 'How badly has that article affected us?'

'Brock Racing has already informed me they will be going with another driver, but they won't make the announcement immediately. They don't want their statement to be overshadowed or seem reactionary. I haven't heard from the other team yet.'

'Funny how this was supposed to help all of us and yet only Aero has benefitted.'

Lukas sat heavily on the couch, phone to his ear, head hanging. Something hard pressed into his thigh. Reaching between the cushions he sat on, he pulled out a gold ring. Katherine's ring. The ring that glinted on her finger when he made love to her on the boat. When he had seen her that very first day.

'It's not over, Lukas.' But Lukas wasn't listening. 'Just give me some—'

He hung up on Dominic, tossing the phone aside as he inspected the piece of jewellery. His heart cracked wide open. And when he looked around, his home had never seemed so full of life and yet so empty, the ghost of happiness haunting every room. Haunting him. He missed Katherine.

He got off the couch and threw the ring across the room with a shout. It hit the glass wall with a loud clang then clattered to the floor somewhere unseen.

'Fuck!' he yelled. In pain. In frustration. In anger at her and himself. He didn't want to miss her. She'd hurt him. Made him believe that he didn't have to be alone anymore. Made him believe that he had found someone who understood him. He'd been starting to think that she loved him and he'd been willing to be patient with her. To let her come to the realisation on her own. To let her decide if she wanted to take a chance on him, because now he realised that he'd been willing to do the same.

For a smart man he was very stupid.

He should never have let down his guard with a journalist.

He walked across the room and retrieved the ring, which had rolled under some furniture. It was a simple, antique fede ring. A ring for friendship. Well, the media certainly wasn't his friend. Katherine's article was proof of that.

But would she have written those things if she had known you?

There was no way to know.

He wasn't aware of any other driver who'd had a journalist force their way into their life like this, just to get more information. More clout. But he'd also never embraced the media like the other drivers had. A decision he could now see made him more enigmatic and fed people's desperate desire to know more, made photographers and journalists more hungry for a picture or a story.

As long as he was a driver, nothing would change. Maybe *he* would have to—maybe he needed to give a bit of himself to the public to satisfy them in order to have the privacy he craved. He didn't know if he could change that much.

Lukas dropped the ring into his pyjama pants pocket and walked out shirtless onto the high terrace. The cold took his breath away, but it was nice to have the physical discomfort. At least it lessened the urgency of his emotional upheaval.

He looked out at the streets of Monaco. In a few months he could be racing along them. The thought didn't fill him with happiness.

Is driving what you're really passionate about?

He loved racing but, no, driving wasn't making him happy anymore. He had more days filled with frustration and anxiety than exhilaration. He wanted to win championships. He was going to make no difference in a backmarker team. The only reason he wanted to stay on the grid was to make his family's sacrifices worth something. So that he wasn't just the selfish ass who robbed his parents of a good life together. But was that enough of a reason to keep racing? Was that a healthy reason?

He examined all the decisions he had made recently. This obsession with driving had made him ignore his principles. He'd agreed to pretend to date someone. He hadn't dated in three years and then only did so to deceive the world. Regardless of what Katherine had done to him or what he felt for her, he'd used her.

This wasn't the man he was.

He was honest. He had integrity. He couldn't let this quest for a drive change him.

But he didn't have to drive to remain in the sport.

You have so much knowledge…such an understanding of the car and the craft that even from a technical aspect you could make a difference.

Lukas leaned his elbows on the glass balustrade, the cold wind ruffling his hair. It hurt to think about Katherine, but a sense of peace settled on him as he thought about the team principal position that he hadn't yet turned down.

Katherine had been right about so much that night at dinner. And about one thing in that heinous article: He did have a wealth of knowledge. He could develop a team. He would have the power to make a difference. To influence decisions. To ensure that the right talent was in the seat without screwing over entire careers. He could make the team what he wanted it to be. He could take all that interest in his name, in him and make it work for the team. For him. There would be a lot of media attention as a team principal but nowhere near as bad as being the star of the team. It was a massive responsibility but without the lens of desperation of wanting to remain a racer, he realised that maybe leading a team was exactly where he should be.

He went back inside and retrieved his phone from the couch, then dialled a number he never thought he would actually use.

'It's Lukas Jäger. I'm accepting your offer of team principal.'

CHAPTER NINETEEN

THE TRACK WAS a hive of activity. Thousands of fans streamed in a continuous line, wearing sunglasses and hats to protect them from the bright Australian mid-March sun. High-powered engines revved until they were practically screaming before being taken to a low growl. Quick short whines of wheel guns punctuated the air.

The first race weekend of the season.

It was only Thursday but that didn't mean that they were in for a quiet day. Drivers were being interviewed in fan zones, support races had practice and qualifying sessions, new drivers had to receive camera time, inserts were being filmed, and drivers and team principals had to hold press conferences.

Team principals like Lukas.

The man she had lost her heart to, the man she had hurt, who wouldn't take her calls or answer her messages. Katherine had tried for weeks before she'd been forced to give up. Every time she'd reached out and he'd rejected her, she'd felt a stab through her heart.

Give him time, Kittykat, her father had said. *Just don't give up.*

But she had to. She'd lost him.

She was on her way back to the Aero broadcast area

when she saw Lukas talking to a group of journalists, most of them from European publications. Lukas talking to the media wasn't unusual. He's always had contractual obligations to fulfil. But Lukas in a grey-and-gold-collared team shirt talking to the media with a smile was.

Katherine watched him from afar. There was no scowl on his face. His body language was open, he was talking with his hands.

He was being friendly to the people he disliked.

Except for her.

Earlier in the paddock, she had seen that unmistakable golden-brown hair, those storm-grey eyes, that chiselled jaw. Lukas had walked towards her and her heart had skipped a beat. Butterflies had erupted in her belly. Her lips tingled with the need for his. His gaze had locked on hers for a moment. Just a moment when she tried to think of everything she wanted to say in those calls and texts. Everything she wanted to do to make her betrayal up to him.

'Lukas,' she had tried to say but it had come out strangled.

He had turned around and walked away.

Katherine was unable to get the image out of her head, even now as she joined her colleagues. When she was informed that they would be interviewing Lukas next, a thrill ran through her body. He would be close to her; he'd be forced to face her.

When he approached, she was ready, mic in hand, heart pounding in her chest.

Every step he took towards her felt like a piece of her was coming home. And when he joined them, she said, 'Hello, Lukas.'

But he didn't respond to her. Instead, he addressed everyone generally. 'This is a little bit different, isn't it?'

'Definitely,' James, the longest-serving presenter said. 'Not seeing you in a race suit is going to take some getting used to.'

'Well, I've swapped one suit for another,' Lukas joked. He *joked*.

And when the camera light turned red, he continued being charming and friendly. Was this the same man she had fallen in love with?

'What was the press conference like this morning, with Thomas Dudek also in attendance?' Katherine asked. Of course, the drama would appeal to fans but also, she was genuinely concerned about how that experience might have affected Lukas. He wouldn't even look at here, so asking was the only way she would know. It wouldn't be his words that told her anything—it would be his body. His eyes.

Lukas glanced at her so quickly before looking away, almost as if to look at her was poisonous. 'Thomas runs a team as do I now. He doesn't get a say in my team and neither do I have a say in his, but we do share a passion for the sport, and we will have to interact from time to time. Perhaps he made some questionable decisions when it came to me as a driver, but he did so for his team. And just because I'm not driving doesn't mean I can't take a team to a championship.'

That told her plenty. Of course, he was hurt having to see the man who had ended his career so heartlessly, but Lukas was trying his best to be diplomatic.

'We're different people,' Lukas continued, 'and will make different decisions.'

Meaning he would not be as unscrupulous as his previous boss.

'And do you think you can take a team as small as this to a championship?' James asked.

'Absolutely. We have to be realistic about our goals and the team is very new, but every team started somewhere, and we just have to be mindful to make the right decisions that will take us in the direction of those goals,' Lukas answered.

He answered every question without snark, without complaint and when James thanked him, Lukas handed back the mic, turned around and walked away without sparing Katherine a second glance. She could have been anyone. She could have been invisible and her already aching heart shattered like the most fragile glass.

Katherine handed the mic off to someone—she didn't really notice who it was—removed the transmitter and all the cables from her clothes, handing those off too, and walked away.

CHAPTER TWENTY

KATHERINE WAITED INSIDE a room filled with charcoal-grey tables and chairs. She was surrounded by three walls of black glass while the back wall was a glossy gold and the floors were light, tying the space together perfectly.

She had never been this anxious in a team motor home and had never been left alone. Journalists weren't usually unaccompanied, but the team had seen fit to let her stay.

So now she waited. She hoped and prayed that Lukas would see her. She had already been waiting awhile. Almost everyone she had initially seen here had left to perform their functions, but she wouldn't leave. Not until she spoke to Lukas.

After an age, he entered the hospitality area talking to a tall, broad, blond man with wire-framed glasses on his patrician nose. The logo of Command Technologies, a well-known tech company, on his shirt. Her instinct was to find out what he was doing here, but she ignored it. She wasn't here for work. She was drawing a line.

'Lukas.' She tried to keep her voice light, maintain perfect composure that wavered slightly when he looked at her. For a moment she thought she saw longing in his eyes, but it was gone faster than it appeared. 'Would it be possible to have a word?'

Lukas looked her over, processing her request before turning to the man and shaking his hand. 'Thank you for stopping by. We'll be in contact soon.'

'Definitely. Vortex Command Racing is going to be the start of great things for us, Jäger.'

Lukas smiled. It wasn't one of the heart-stopping smiles he had given her in Monaco, this one was practiced. Cordial and charming. No one would know the difference but her.

'I couldn't agree more, Matthew,' Lukas said and watched the man leave. The door had only just closed when he rounded on Katherine. 'We can talk in my office.' He led her through the back doorway to a set of stairs. 'I don't need you making a scene.'

'I would never do that.' It hurt to hear him think that way of her.

'Really?' They reached the top and he held a glass door open for her to step into. 'What would you call all those calls and messages, then?'

'Wanting to talk.'

He closed the door, sealing them inside a small, impeccably neat office. He had two visitor chairs on one side of his desk and a large comfortable-looking one on the other, but he didn't sit, nor did he invite Katherine to do so.

'You had plenty of opportunities to talk but when it mattered, you didn't.'

'Can you at least say my name?' It had been months since she'd heard him use it and all through the day he wouldn't acknowledge her. Now he was talking to her yet still wouldn't address her. It was tearing her up.

'Why?' he asked in a hard tone.

'Because I need to hear it.'

He shook his head and walked past her to stand at the glass wall looking out at the sunny paddock.

'Why are you here, Katherine?'

Every cell in her body came to life at the sound of her name on his tongue and she couldn't savour it. 'To ask for your forgiveness.'

'My forgiveness,' he scoffed.

'I asked them to scrap the article and they ran it anyway without telling me. You know this. I tried to fix it, Lukas. Yes, I should have told you about it, but I never meant to hurt your feelings.'

'Don't lie.' He turned towards her. Sadness, disappointment, hurt written all over his face. 'That's not true. Because the fact is you did write that article. You planned it, did research, thought of the words—the best words to get your point across—and then reread it before you submitted it.'

Katherine didn't know how to defend herself against that because he had a point. There was always a lot of consideration in her writing. 'You said you'd already seen all that I'd written, that we moved past the hate. Did you mean that?'

'You don't get to ask me that.' Despite his even tone, there was anger in his eyes. 'Are you proud of it?'

'No!' Katherine replied instantly. It was the least proud she had ever been of herself. No matter how disappointed Lukas was in her, it would never compare to how she felt about herself when she thought about how she had let her mistaken hate of him colour her judgement.

'When you first wrote it, Katherine,' he said slowly, 'when you typed it up and put it on an email that you sent to your editor, were you proud of it?'

Her insides squirmed. How she wished she could go

back to that moment and do it all over again because she had been proud. Exceptionally so. 'Yes,' she confessed. 'But, Lukas, it isn't like that. I've changed!' She marched up to the man she loved and grabbed a fistful of his shirt, but his arms hung limply by his sides. He looked down at her, not pushing her away, but not touching her either. And even though it was the worst pain imaginable, she continued, 'I see you for who you are. I was wrong and I'm sorry, Lukas. I'm so sorry!'

He stepped back, forcing her to let go. 'You don't get it. You did believe the things you wrote about me even if you no longer do. You were willing to believe the worst about me without ever talking to me or finding out the truth. You can only believe the worst about someone if you *want* to.'

'Lukas…'

'And you didn't just believe it,' he went on. 'You kept telling the world. You wanted everyone to think of me as you did. And even though you attacked me over and over again, I never said a bad thing about you, Of course, I vented to Dominic or my father because I am human after all. But not publicly, ever. Not once, Katherine.'

Her eyes welled with tears because he was right.

'I never once did the things you did.' He walked to the door and grabbed onto the handle about to pull it open but she stopped him.

Tears she couldn't control streamed down her cheeks. 'I'm not doing the column anymore.'

She could see that caught his attention. He let go of the door handle and turned towards her even though he remained at a distance.

'I'm done with opinion pieces.'

'What would you like me to say?' he asked plainly.

'I just wanted you to know.' Maybe then he could see that she was committed to being better.

'I never wanted you to give up your job, Katherine. I know what your success means to you. Means for your family. And I've been in the racing world a long time, I understand the need for you in it. The media is an important part of the sport, but it was never going to work between us. Don't give up your dream for me when we're never going to be together.'

'I just need you to forgive me,' Katherine pleaded.

'And then what? Hmm?' Lukas crossed his arms. 'How does it help? Where do we go from there?'

'Even if you can't be with me, maybe if you can forgive me we can find a way to at least be friends. I confided in you, Lukas. I trust you. I can't lose you from my life.'

But all he did was shake his head. Katherine was breaking apart. Willing to settle for the crumbs of the affection he once had for her, but he wouldn't budge.

'I said I wanted you on the boat but I didn't want to think about why I wanted *you* so much, Lukas. I want all of you. I love you, but I'll settle for anything you're willing to give me.'

He pressed his back to the door, dropping his head back to rest against the glass, his neck exposed. He closed his eyes. Katherine wanted to scream for him to open them. Open them and look at her.

'Love doesn't hurt like you hurt me.' He ran his fingers through his hair as he said softly to himself, 'Maybe it does. What would I know about it?'

The woman he'd wanted to marry had left him because he was too zealous about protecting their privacy; his mother had left and kept punishing him for choices he hadn't made. Everyone Lukas loved had hurt him, including her. Katherine hated that fact. She wanted to wrap him in her arms and comfort him. Wanted to hear him say he forgave her and that he needed her. 'I know I hurt you, but I'm willing to make it up to you every single day, Lukas.'

Then he did look at her, and she thought she might combust. 'Why should I take you back?'

'Because you still love me. You loved me on the boat, and you love me now. If you didn't you wouldn't be hearing me out. You could have exposed our fake relationship—even though it wasn't fake to me—and ruined me, but you didn't. And I know I saw pride in your eyes when you saw me with the other presenters. It was so brief, but it was there.'

He pulled himself up to standing, shaking his head and pressing his thumb and finger to his eyes. Katherine saw his jaw twitch from gritting his teeth. His throat bobbed in a hard swallow and when he finally dropped his hand from his eyes and spoke, his voice was rough. Low and raw. Bleeding all the pain she could see in his stormy gaze.

'Of course I love you, Katherine. I can't turn my feelings off. I've never felt about anyone the way I felt about you, but I don't know how to trust you. It's just best if we have nothing to do with each other. It will be easier for both of us and save us the heartache.'

'Please, Lukas,' she cried.

'You can take a minute to compose yourself. Goodbye, Katherine,' he said softly. Solemnly.

She thought she had reached the bottom of the well when it came to this pain, but hope had kept her afloat. Now she was drowning. Couldn't breathe because every breath had shards in it, ripping her on the inside. Lukas, the only man she had ever truly loved, was gone.

CHAPTER TWENTY-ONE

KATHERINE NEEDED TO find a quiet place to breathe. To be alone. Somewhere she could hurt without being seen.

'Kat?'

She startled at the voice, thinking she had found solitude between the team trucks.

'Dominic.' He looked at her with sympathy, which made her feel worse. 'I'm not the best company right now.'

'Me neither, but I don't think the best is what either of us needs.'

It was only then that Katherine realised Dominic must be facing a very different dynamic with Lukas too. Lukas didn't need a manager anymore, and Dominic had been with him for almost twenty years.

'How are you holding up?'

'Could be better.' He shrugged. 'Don't get me wrong, I'm happy for Lukas. I didn't want him to end his career at the back of the field. But when your friend and client keeps something that big from you, it makes you question a few things. Like the wisdom of making him pretend to date a journalist.'

'You were trying to do your best for him.' Katherine leaned against the grey-and-gold truck. 'But you're right, maybe it was a mistake. How is he?' Dominic was the only means she had to get any news on how Lukas was *really* doing.

'Angry,' Dominic replied.

'At me?' It was nearly a whisper.

'You, himself, me. But here's the thing about Lukas, he can be quite fair even when he's upset. I mean, he didn't kick me out when I visited him on Christmas Day. Though he did put me to work.'

'What do you mean?'

Dominic chuckled sadly. 'He made me pack away Christmas decorations in the lounge. He didn't help at all. Didn't even look at them. He only joined me after I'd put everything into storage.'

He wouldn't even look at them. That's how much he hated Katherine now.

Lounge.

'Only the lounge? What about the tree in his bedroom?' Katherine's heart beat frantically waiting for the answer as if her life depended on it. Well, maybe not her life, but certainly her happiness.

'I don't know. I didn't go up there and he said nothing.'

Could he have kept that one reminder of her? The same man who walked away from her twice that day. Unlikely. It probably went into the trash. Her vision became blurry but she couldn't cry. Not at the track. Not in front of Dominic.

She swallowed hard, but her throat was closing. 'I need to…' She looked around. Eyes darting from one point to the next. Searching for an answer. 'I need to make this right.'

But how? Lukas didn't want to be with her. He didn't want to see her. By the sounds of it he was pushing Dominic away in his anger. Who was Lukas confiding in? She had gone straight to her father for comfort, but Lukas couldn't do the same.

Whether a future with him was lost or not, Katherine needed Lukas to be okay. She needed him to have someone he could lean on, so he wasn't so alone.

She was hit with a wave of inspiration and knew exactly what she had to do.

'I have to go!'

CHAPTER TWENTY-TWO

IT WAS THE morning of race day.

Lukas lay on his hotel room bed fully dressed. The image of a pleading Katherine in his head as it had been for two days.

Every atom in his body had begged him to take her in his arms. He'd wanted so badly to cave to her because he missed her. Every day without her was an ache in his chest that never faded. But the fact was that they couldn't be together. Offering her comfort wouldn't help them move on. And they both needed to.

The snowflake was still in his bedroom. He wanted to get rid of it but couldn't. So, it sat there taunting him every morning. He'd still looked for her at the track every day, albeit from a distance. When he'd failed to find her at all these past two days, he still couldn't help but worry about her absence.

'Why can't I stop loving you!' he said angrily to himself.

He had to concede that he was never going to stop thinking about her, but it was time to head to the track. He had work to do. But a knock on the door stopped him.

He opened it without checking to see who it was. They were a new team and he had made sure that their accommodation was kept a secret. If anyone needed him, it was likely someone from the hotel or team.

He was entirely unprepared for the person staring back at him.

'Mutter,' he said in shock.

'Hello, Lukas.'

He stood there, staring at the woman with sharply cut blond hair. She was a whole head shorter than him, with the same storm-grey eyes. Eyes that held apprehension.

His mother.

Curiosity warred with suspicion, but the former won out. He opened the door wider to allow her in. Door handle still in hand, as he watched his mother sit at the small, round, dark wood table.

Mechanically, as if his joints were in the process of seizing, he closed the door and approached Berta Jäger. Lukas was always certain about what he wanted to do. When racing was the wrong choice, he was still certain he wanted to do it. When he'd eventually let go of that obsession and considered the team principal move, he was certain of that choice. Even when he made Katherine leave his home, he was certain that was the end. But now, with his mother in his room and with no idea why she'd come, Lukas wasn't certain anymore. He didn't know if he should join her or keep standing or hover at the door. Should he demand to know why she was there or just be grateful that she was?

He didn't like being indecisive. He was used to making quick decisions, to reacting in two-tenths of a second. So he shrugged on the persona that made him so successful in his sport and approached the table.

'What are you doing here?' He kept his voice polite, but there was no missing the demand in his tone.

'I've come to see my son,' Berta said carefully.

He eased himself into the opposite chair, laying his arms on the padded armrests. 'You never have before. Why now?'

He could see his mother thinking of a response, but he didn't want that. He wanted anything she said to be completely unfiltered. After Katherine and the article and the fake relationship, he didn't have it in him to be patient with anything but the truth.

'I want the real reason.'

'A young woman came to see me this weekend and she brought me here, but she wanted to keep it a secret.'

Katherine.

'Who was it?' He held his breath almost praying for his mother to say her name.

'Katherine Ward.'

Lukas closed his eyes tightly. This was why he hadn't seen her for two days. She had flown to Salzburg. It was a long flight to get from Australia to Austria. She could have missed the whole race weekend. She *had* missed most of it. Why did she do this for him?

'She didn't want you to know but suspected maybe a talk would help us both.'

What did that mean? Had Katherine confronted her parents? Lukas found himself wishing he'd been with her if she had. Just like he wished she was with him now, which was ridiculous after she had hurt him.

'Is that what you want? To talk?' Lukas refused to allow himself any expectations. He knew what he was guilty of, he also knew how badly he'd wanted his mother in his life growing up and how much it had stung when she refused to see him as an adult.

'I don't really know, Lukas.' His mother wrung her fingers.

'Then why are you here? Why did you leave Salzburg? It's a long flight.'

She stopped fidgeting, folded her hands on the table and looked her son square in the eye. 'I guess I'm here because that young lady gave me a lot to think about.'

Lukas wanted to know every word that Katherine had said but couldn't ask. He was dying for any kind of information about the past few months and maybe he was regretting the fact that he didn't take her call. But he also didn't want to hurt himself by talking to her and making the chasm in his chest yawn wider.

'Go on.'

'She made me realise that I've hurt you. You see, Lukas, I had a great deal of resentment, and I put that on you instead of where it should have lain.'

'And where was that?'

'With your father,' she said without missing a beat.

'Don't. Don't blame him when he never did a thing wrong.' His father had sacrificed everything so that Lukas could have the kind of future he was enjoying.

'Then where do you feel the blame lies?' she asked, leaning forward just a little.

'With me,' Lukas said easily. He knew the truth and no one could tell him otherwise. 'It was my fault that he had to work two jobs. My fault that you were unhappy. My fault that you left. I know that. But I have been trying to make it up to you. To give you the life you wanted to have.'

His mother's eyes softened a fraction. 'I let you believe that, didn't I?' She shook her head sadly. 'Katherine told me I would need to take responsibility for what I had done to you and I see now that she's right.'

Lukas didn't know how to respond.

I'm not doing the column anymore.

He knew Katherine was trying to do the same—to take responsibility—but it didn't change things. He was a private person; he would make her miserable. And what about when she had to report on his team? Chances were they wouldn't have any big results for at least the first half of the season, how would he respond when she had to be critical?

'Your father could have said no when you wanted to race after that first time he took you to the track. Do you remember that day?'

Lukas shook his head. Those memories were blurry. He remembered getting into the kart and the feeling but not too much else.

'One of the families that he used to get your tyres from were getting rid of their kart, so your father offered to buy it from them. They gave it to him in exchange for him servicing their son's kart for the next year. His labour would be free, and he agreed. I wasn't happy. That was money we could have used, but your father took you to the track and you listened so carefully to the safety instructions and what to do. Then you got to drive. You went slowly at first because they told you to. They said the tyres would be cold and you did everything as instructed. We thought you would enjoy yourself and then we would go home but the next lap you went faster and the one after that, faster still. I remember it so clearly, Lukas, people started watching *you*. Not anyone else. It was like you were born to race. Afterwards someone told your father he should let you race, and you asked him if you could. You were so excited and he said yes. He didn't talk to me first. He made the decision.

'When we got home he spoke to me about what changes we would have to make to support your racing and I thought it was unnecessary. The chance of you getting into Alpha One was so small, what would we have for all that investment? And the days got tough after that, Lukas.'

'I know. I was there. I could see the toll my racing was taking,' Lukas said softly.

'I wanted a better life, and I resented your father for not allowing us to have that but I also didn't want to blame him, because I loved him still, so I blamed you. My son.' Lukas could see the shame in her drooped shoulders. In the fact she wouldn't look at him. 'But I watched you with pride, Lukas. I know it might not seem like it makes sense. I don't feel like I deserve to have you in my life now when you're successful.'

'That's why you don't want to see me. Why you're making it so hard for me to take care of you.' Lukas wondered then if Katherine would one day face the same barrier with her parents, because just like him, she wanted to take care of them. Make their lives easier.

She understood you.

She hurt me.

Others wrote hurtful and false things about you too. Why was Katherine's so much worse?

That was a good question. It made him really look at their past, how much attention he'd paid to her, the fact that he tried to make sure her producer knew that him not wanting to talk to her was *not* her fault. The fact that he mentioned to Aero that they should hire her. That he paid so much more attention to her articles than anyone else's. Her articles got under his skin because he had set her apart. He even called her 'Katherine' when no one else did.

'Yes,' his mother said, startling Lukas out of the reverie he had fallen into. He'd almost forgotten the question he'd asked her. 'I'm sorry, Lukas.' She reached across the table and placed her hand on his. The contact felt so alien, so unfamiliar, but he had craved it for so long. 'Can you ever forgive me?'

'Yes.' He didn't have to think about it because that was the path back to having family in his life. He had no siblings. He was certain it was his fault his mother had chosen never to start another family, because what if they were like him? His father was dead. All he had was his mother and he so desperately wanted her in his life. 'I forgive you, but do you forgive me?'

'There's nothing to forgive. It wasn't your fault. You're not selfish. You were just a child with a dream, and you made it come true. I should have supported you. I can't go back and undo the past but maybe if you let me, I could be at the track today?'

'I have always wanted that,' Lukas confessed. A small piece of the scattered puzzle his heart had broken into clicked back into place. The rest remained broken.

'These scars you carry should not have been yours to bear, *liebling*. Let the world look at you because they will find a strong, kind, determined man. Katherine saw you and she fell in love with you.'

'I don't know if Katherine and I can be together.' But, good Lord did he want that.

Not letting go of his hand, she brought her other hand up to cup his cheek and gave him a sad, watery smile. 'Everyone makes mistakes. I'm sure you made them too. You just forgave me after a lifetime of mistakes I made. Maybe you could do the same for her?' Her tone was gentle.

Maybe he could forgive Katherine. After all, he was excited about this new journey in the sport he so loved. It didn't matter to him now who was in his seat at his old team. He didn't care. If someone had asked him what his greatest goal was this weekend, he would say to have two cars finish the race and maybe score a point or two.

'I want to,' he confessed to his mother. 'But…'

'Lukas, do you love her?'

'With my soul.'

His mother got off her chair and went to stand beside him. He looked up at her, unable to remember when he last had a memory like it, and then her arms went around him, pressing him to her middle. A hug he had craved after she had left him and his father. So he held on to his mother, taking all the affection she was offering, wondering if it was too good to be true and would all be taken away in the blink of an eye.

'A love like this isn't easily found. She's brave, *liebling*. She told me things I didn't want to hear. She brought us together and didn't want the credit. She's as determined as you are. From what I can see, as selfless.'

His mother was right. Lukas would never have known Katherine had gone to Salzburg if his mother hadn't told him. Who did that? Who went out of their way to fix something so broken in someone's life.

Someone in love.

He let go of his mother almost in a daze.

'I'm going to go. I can see you have a lot to think about.'

Lukas gave his mother one last hug before walking her to the door. 'I'll see you later.'

It was unreal that he was able to say those words. He only could because of Katherine.

'Definitely.' His mother smiled and closed the door behind her, leaving him with thoughts only of Katherine. She did love him. She showed him as much at Christmas, with the snowflake, his mother and giving up the column.

She was so afraid of sacrificing her career like her

mother did and yet she let her column go for him. She was willing to make changes to accommodate him. Showed him commitment. So why couldn't they be together? Why couldn't he trust her?

Love was such a risk to the life she wanted but she told him she loved him.

As if a light had switched on, Lukas could see how idiotic he was being. He needed to find her. They wouldn't be miserable together; they were miserable without each other.

He grabbed his keys and rushed out of the room, letting the door slam on their past mistakes. There was a future to fight for.

CHAPTER TWENTY-THREE

LUKAS STOOD IN front of a closed hotel room door. A quick text to Erin was all it had taken to find out where the Aero TV team was staying. And then he'd run. He'd run down to the street where he saw the back end of a tram disappearing into the distance. He could have taken his car but the only route he knew well was going from the hotel to the track. He never saw much of the city as a driver and was somehow seeing even less now. But from where he stood, he could see part of the building peeking through others…so he kept running until he made it here.

He knocked rapidly at the door and when it opened, a tired, puffy-eyed Katherine answered.

'Lukas,' she breathed. Eyes wide as if he was the last person she expected.

'Is that my…'

She pulled the hem of the shirt, looking down at the white cotton. 'I found it in my bag after we left Lapland. I wanted to—' She stopped herself. 'Do you want it back?' Her lip trembled.

But Lukas needed to hear what she refused to say. 'You wanted to…?'

Katherine clenched her jaw and straightened her spine, looking him in the eye. He loved that fire. 'I wanted to have your scent close to me because I missed you. I still miss you.'

'I miss you too, Katherine. Can we talk?' He was very aware that she hadn't invited him into her room, seeing her bloodshot eyes and red nose it wasn't hard to guess why.

Katherine didn't budge. He could see her warring emotions. She still wanted him but his refusal before had hurt. Katherine wasn't the crying type. She had taught herself to be controlled but he had brought tears to her eyes several times and for that, he would never forgive himself.

'Please,' he added.

She stepped aside and in he walked. Her laptop was open on the bed, her phone displaying a thread of texts beside it. Scribbled notes on a writing pad lay on the table. The television was switched on but muted and on the bedside table a small pile of crumpled tissues.

Katherine closed the door and joined him, keeping her distance but he didn't want that. He reached for her hand and tried to pull her closer, but Katherine would only move so much.

'You said goodbye, Lukas.'

'I did but I shouldn't have. It was an idiotic thing to do when I love you.'

Katherine didn't say anything. He'd admitted to loving her before but had still pushed her away. This distance was his fault.

'You were right, I do love you. I never stopped. You're my first and last thought every day, Katherine. I wake up and look at the snowflake. It's the last thing I see before I close my eyes. I couldn't move it. I couldn't get rid of it. It hurts to see it, because you're not there, but the thought of losing the one thing that ties me to you hurts so much more.'

'Dominic said you made him take down the decorations.' Her eyes welled up again. A tear danced on the edge of her lashes but she was trying not to let it fall. She'd let herself be vulnerable with him and now she was trying so hard not to be. He'd let her keep her guard up if that was what she needed but he would show her that it was okay to let go. That he would let his own barriers down so maybe she would too.

'I did. I was hurt. I couldn't enter that room and see the reminders of you. Of a moment when we were happy. But, Katherine, that isn't close to as happy as we could be. And I want to be happy with you.'

'But you said—'

'I hadn't coped well with seeing you. I still blamed you for everything, but I've had time to think and I want to try again.'

Katherine pulled her hand from his and moved to stand by the table. She tried to speak but nothing came out, so she swallowed hard and tried again. 'What's changed?'

Everything.

Lukas went to the window. He respected Katherine's need for space but that didn't stop him craving her closeness. His body constantly reaching for hers and maybe she felt the same, because even though she didn't directly look at him, her body still pivoted towards his.

'My mother came to see me this morning.' Katherine's eyes snapped to his. He needed her to see his earnestness. 'And I realised how much you love me and how much I can trust you. I confided a lot in you that you could have used but you didn't. Instead, you did the impossible and brought my mother back into my life. I don't know what you told her, but I can imagine how much you would have had to open up to a stranger to make her listen to you.' He went to Katherine then, whose tears refused to be controlled any longer, and he kissed the wetness away. 'That was a long way to go. You could have missed the first race of the season.'

'I would do it again for you, Lukas.'

'Katherine,' he breathed, his thumbs gently caressing her cheeks. 'I may not have liked or agreed with how you went about trying to get rid of the article, but you did try. I didn't make you feel like you could confide in me about your job. I had a very black and white view on the media— they were the enemy and that drove a wedge between us. So I also have to bear some of the responsibility. It was wrong to put it all on you.'

'We both made mistakes,' Katherine said. Lukas didn't know if she had realised it, but she'd moved closer to him. He couldn't describe the elation that little movement brought him.

'We did. I'm trying to do better. I'm learning to give a little more of myself to the media and it has brought me some space in my private life. Though, without you, I don't need it.'

'Why?'

'Because without you, I'm not living, Katherine. I'm existing, and there is a very big difference in that.'

'I'm not living without you either.'

Lukas pulled her against his body. His fingertips tangling in her fiery red hair. His palm cupping her cheek. *This* right here was home. With his heart pounding frantically because that was just the effect her touch had on him. His spirit calm because she was close.

'Love is scary, I know that, and I know how difficult it would have been for you to admit you love me. But I promise you, we will be stronger for being together. I will support your career wherever you choose to go. Loving me will never mean you could lose your dream. Never.'

'I know that, Lukas. You made me see that my career didn't have to be my whole life. That with you I could have success *and* love. What you did for me... I'm sorry I used my position at Aero to hurt you.'

He had wanted that apology for so long and, while he appreciated it, Lukas found that he didn't really care anymore. There were more important things than being a driver or worrying about how the world saw him. He only cared what Katherine thought.

'That's behind us. And while I think you're incredible on *Track Talk*, I think you should get your column back too. You're good. People need to hear from *you*.'

'I love you, Lukas.'

'I love you too, Katherine. Will you let me show you how much?' After months of being without her and having her body so close to his now, Lukas was suffocating, in need of the air that was her lips on his. He was cold, desperate for the heat of her skin on his.

'Yes.'

So he kissed her. He kissed her in apology and as a new beginning. He kissed her in a promise of love and show of devotion. He kissed her with his heart and soul. Her arms tightened around him and his tongue worshipped at her mouth. He never wanted to stop. He wanted this feeling every day until the end of time.

Katherine broke the kiss with a smile, but she didn't pull away. He could feel the puffs of her staccato breath on his lips and he wanted more.

'This doesn't mean you get special treatment. I still have a job to do,' she joked.

'I wouldn't dream of it, but if you could keep my personal life out of it, I would appreciate it. You see, my wife is going to be extremely well-known.'

Katherine laughed. 'Your wife, huh?'

'I'm hoping.' He kissed her briefly again. 'I'm never letting her go.'

'I like the sound of that,' Katherine replied.

* * * * *

If Snowed-In Enemies *left you wanting more,
why not explore these other passionate stories
from Bella Mason?*

Secretly Pregnant by the Tycoon
Their Diamond Ring Ruse
His Chosen Queen
Strictly Forbidden Boss
Pregnant Before 'I Do'

Available now!

Get up to 4 Free Books!

We'll send you 2 free books from each series you try PLUS a free Mystery Gift.

FREE
Value Over
$25

Both the **Harlequin Presents** and **Harlequin Medical Romance** series feature exciting stories of passion and drama.

YES! Please send me 2 FREE novels from Harlequin Presents or Harlequin Medical Romance and my FREE gift (gift is worth about $10 retail). After receiving them, if I don't wish to receive any more books, I can return the shipping statement marked "cancel." If I don't cancel, I will receive 6 brand-new larger-print novels every month and be billed just $7.19 each in the U.S., or $7.99 each in Canada, or 4 brand-new Harlequin Medical Romance Larger-Print books every month and be billed just $7.19 each in the U.S. or $7.99 each in Canada, a savings of 20% off the cover price. It's quite a bargain! Shipping and handling is just 50¢ per book in the U.S. and $1.25 per book in Canada.* I understand that accepting the 2 free books and gift places me under no obligation to buy anything. I can always return a shipment and cancel at any time. The free books and gift are mine to keep no matter what I decide.

Choose one:
☐ **Harlequin Presents Larger-Print** (176/376 BPA G36Y)
☐ **Harlequin Medical Romance** (171/371 BPA G36Y)
☐ **Or Try Both!** (176/376 & 171/371 BPA G36Z)

Name (please print)

Address   Apt. #

City   State/Province   Zip/Postal Code

Email: Please check this box ☐ if you would like to receive newsletters and promotional emails from Harlequin Enterprises ULC and its affiliates. You can unsubscribe anytime.

> Mail to the **Harlequin Reader Service:**
> **IN U.S.A.:** P.O. Box 1341, Buffalo, NY 14240-8531
> **IN CANADA:** P.O. Box 603, Fort Erie, Ontario L2A 5X3

Want to explore our other series or interested in ebooks? Visit www.ReaderService.com or call 1-800-873-8635.

---

*Terms and prices subject to change without notice. Prices do not include sales taxes, which will be charged (if applicable) based on your state or country of residence. Canadian residents will be charged applicable taxes. Offer not valid in Quebec. This offer is limited to one order per household. Books received may not be as shown. Not valid for current subscribers to the Harlequin Presents or Harlequin Medical Romance series. All orders subject to approval. Credit or debit balances in a customer's account(s) may be offset by any other outstanding balance owed by or to the customer. Please allow 4 to 6 weeks for delivery. Offer available while quantities last.

Your Privacy—Your information is being collected by Harlequin Enterprises ULC, operating as Harlequin Reader Service. For a complete summary of the information we collect, how we use this information and to whom it is disclosed, please visit our privacy notice located at https://corporate. harlequin.com/privacy-notice. Notice to California Residents – Under California law, you have specific rights to control and access your data. For more information on these rights and how to exercise them, visit https://corporate.harlequin.com/california-privacy. For additional information for residents of other U.S. states that provide their residents with certain rights with respect personal data, visit https://corporate.harlequin.com/other-state-residents-privacy-rights/.

HPHM25